Sometimes...

A Play

Kevin Cowdall

Sometimes . . .

Copyright © Kevin Cowdall 2002

ISBN: 9798371184627

This paperback edition first published
by Kindle Direct Publishing (KDP) 2022

For all the times
that might have been
and all the people
who might have shared them.

'All the world's a stage,
And all the men and women merely players;
They have their exits and their entrances,
And one man in his time plays many parts . . .'

William Shakespeare – *As You Like It*,
Act II, Scene VII

CHARACTERS
(In order of appearance)

JULIET: Donald's assistant and partner. American, mid-twenties.

DONALD TRAVERS, CBE: Highly successful author, poet, playwright. Fifty(ish).

SIMON COURTNEY: Donald's agent. Early thirties.

DOCTOR ROGER BRAITHWAITE: Donald's GP and an old friend. Late forties.

SUSAN TRAVERS: Donald's daughter. An actress, mid-twenties.

ASLAN BASINDAH: Susan's boyfriend. An actor. Asian, mid-twenties.

ROBIN BENJAMIN: Secretary of the Winsonian Society of Philadelphia. African-American, late thirties.

HOWARD MCPHERSONN: Director of the Winsonian Society of Philadelphia. American, mid-sixties.

CHRISTOPHER SAYLE: Donald's solicitor and an old friend. Late forties.

MARTIN OSGOOD: A literary correspondent from *The Times*. Mid-twenties.

KATHERINE TRAVERS: Donald's ex-wife. A successful actress, mid-forties.

SET

The story takes place throughout on the patio area of Donald's house, situated on the outskirts of a village somewhere in the Home Counties.

The four Acts coincide with the seasons of the year and lighting, characters' clothing, and set decorations, such as potted plants, etc, should reflect the changing time of year.

ACT ONE

Dusk. Early spring. Not too long ago. The patio and upper garden to the rear of a large country house on the outskirts of a village somewhere in the Home Counties. At stage right stands a large wooden garden shed, side on at an angle, the door, window, and skylight of which are all open. To stage left is the main patio area, slightly raised, on which is set a circular wrought iron table and a set of four matching chairs, as if they have been unused for several months. The umbrella which accompanies these is folded and sheathed and has been lent against the wall of the house. The rear of the stage is taken up by the lower rear elevation of the house which should include to the left, a kitchen door, ajar at this point, and an adjacent sash window, which is closed and has the curtains drawn. To the right are a set of French windows, which open onto a lounge. These are also closed at this point and the curtains, likewise, are drawn. JULIET enters from the shed and closes the door behind her on a Yale or similar lock. She is wearing an overcoat, scarf, and cloche hat and is carrying a large cardboard box filled with various unidentifiable items.

JULIET: Sometimes, people ask me how I ever got myself into such a situation – as if I had no say in the matter, as if it were something I had no control over. *(She pauses, setting the box down)* God! If I'd known it would end like this . . . *(She glances around her briefly, shaking her head, then picks the box up again and exits via the kitchen door, closing it behind her)*

Mid-afternoon. A bright, sunny day in early spring, approximately twelve months or so earlier. The scene is as before, although the curtains to the kitchen window and French windows are both now open. The sound of a practiced and steady typing comes from inside the shed, the window and skylight of which are also both open. JULIET enters via the kitchen. She is carrying a handful of envelopes of various colours and sizes, which she is sorting through as she walks.

JULIET: *(Crossing to the shed)* Donald, mail. *(The sound of typing stops)*

DONALD: *(From inside the shed)* How many times must I tell you, you irritating American brat, the word is *post*. Letters are *posted* in a *post*-box to be delivered by a *post*man employed by the *Post* Office.

JULIET: Mrs Wainwright is most definitely a woman, Donald –

DONALD: *(Interrupting) Post*-woman, *post*-person –

JULIET: *(Continuing)* – and she's employed by the Royal Mail.

DONALD: *(After a moment)* Irritating child. *(His hand*

appears from the shed window and JULIET *passes him the pile of envelopes. After a moment the first of these comes flying back through the window, to be followed by a steady stream of them, which* JULIET *seems to be expecting and catches with expert ease)* Bill, circular, bill, circular, circular, bill – I thought I employed you to – Ahah!

JULIET: Something interesting, beloved?

DONALD: Potentially, potentially. White linen-weave envelope with a window – oh, dear!

JULIET: What's wrong?

DONALD: American stamp and *post*mark.

> *(The envelope comes flying through the window)*

JULIET: *(Catching it)* Don't you even want to open it?

> *(The sound of typing begins again. She opens the letter and reads it)*
>
> Donald. Donald!
>
> *(The typing stops)*

DONALD: What is it now?

JULIET: I think you should read this.

DONALD: Why?

JULIET: You've been awarded a, and I quote, 'major literary prize', unquote –

DONALD: Another bloody tin pot. No thank you. *(He starts to type oncemore)*

JULIET: *(Continuing)* – and a cheque for ten thousand dollars.

(The typing stops abruptly)

DONALD: *(After a moment)* What is that in real money?

JULIET: About eight and a half thousand pound.

DONALD: Bloody hell! *(He appears in the doorway of the shed)* Well, carry on! What else does it say?

JULIET: It's from the Winsonian Society of Philadelphia.

DONALD: The whatonian society of where?

JULIET: The Winsonian Society of Philadelphia. *(Reading)* Formed in 1919, the Society aims to recognise and reward the achievements of British and other European writers in the promotion of peace and social, cultural, and political tolerance and understanding.

DONALD: Bloody hell! Anything else?

JULIET: The award is presented on a triennial basis –

DONALD: *(Interrupting)* That means every three years.

JULIET: Don't patronise me or I'll eat the letter.

DONALD: Apologies, sweetness. Continue.

JULIET: The award is presented on a triennial basis for a collection of work which best embodies the spirit of the Society, and takes the form of two mounted doves –

DONALD: *(Interrupting again)* Two pigeons fucking, presumably.

JULIET: I won't tell you again, Donald.

(He gestures magnanimously for her to continue)

Two mounted doves on a mahogany base

encircled by a garland of laurel –

DONALD: Bloody – *(He slaps both hands over his mouth and makes an exaggerated display of composing himself)*

JULIET: Garland of laurel. The recipient will also receive a cheque for ten thousand US dollars or the equivalent in the recipient's national currency. We would be grateful if you would contact the Society at your earliest convenience to let us know if you are willing to accept the award and, if so, that we may make any necessary arrangements for a suitable presentation. Yours sincerely, Robin T. Benjamin, Secretary.
(DONALD raises one hand)
Yes?

DONALD: I have never heard of the Winsonian Society of Philadelphia. As Americans their thought processes are, naturally, beyond any logical reason, but why would they wish to give me money?

JULIET: *(Looking at him archly, then in a broad drawl)* We Yankees have always felt somewhat piteous of our cousins across the water, Mister Travers, Sir. We do like to help in any small way that presents itself. *(She finishes with a grand curtsey)*

DONALD: Irritating brat.

JULIET: Donald, you cannot go on blaming an entire

nation because your stupid ex-wife left you for an American. If you don't want to accept the award, just say so, and I'll let them know, otherwise –

DONALD: *(Interrupting)* My darling, while leaving me may, in itself, have been an act of the grossest stupidity, Katherine was, normally, a woman of above average intelligence. *(He pauses for the expected reaction then continues)* You know, I think I love you most when you have that fire in you eyes –

JULIET: *(Interrupting in turn)* Oh, shut up, you old fart.

DONALD: Do not interrupt, dearest, it is the height of ill manners. While I have no objection in principal to receiving the award, and the money, while not essential, will pay for an acceptable holiday, if nothing else. However, I have no intention of travelling to collect either if I have to go anywhere near California.

JULIET: As you well know, Philadelphia is on the opposite coast, over two and a half thousand miles, and a couple of time zones away. You're just being petulant. If you want, I'll ring this Robin T. Benjamin and see what the arrangements are.

DONALD: Fair enough. Probably some academic old sprout straight out of a Malcolm Bradbury novel. Once you have done that you can rustle up something to eat and open a bottle of wine. We might as well celebrate while I am in a good mood.

(He leads the way toward the kitchen door, JULIET follows. As they near she suddenly pinches his backside with both hands)

JULIET: Why don't we celebrate first and eat afterwards?

DONALD: *(As they disappear indoors)* You are a brazen young hussy.

JULIET: *(Off. Giggling loudly, then with a scream of surprise)* Donald!

Late afternoon. A fortnight or so later. The garden is as before, except that the furniture is now set out, with several sheets of paper scattered over the table and a couple of the chairs. The umbrella is not yet in use. DONALD sits at another of the chairs reading through more papers. He sets down the papers with a sudden grimace, flexes the fingers of his right hand, and massages the upper arm with his other hand. He is clearly in some discomfort, and is unable to continue for a while. The front door bell is heard to ring, followed by the sound of voices from within. Enter JULIET and SIMON via the kitchen door. SIMON is carrying a brown paper bag under one arm

JULIET: *(Calling as they appear)* Donald, it's Simon.

DONALD: *(Composing himself with difficulty before standing)* If you have come for your percentage you are a bit premature, the Yanks are not coming over until July, and awards don't count anyway.

SIMON: Donald, I have come at the earliest possible moment, given my hectic schedule, to congratulate you, and to bring you this by way of celebration. *(He takes a bottle of vintage wine from the bag he has been carrying and offers it to DONALD)* Congratulations! *(He extends his right hand)*

(After a moment's hesitation DONALD ignores the proffered hand-shake and takes the bottle in his left hand)

DONALD: Do sit down, dear boy.

(SIMON takes the chair vacated by DONALD as DONALD examines the label)

This is rather good. You obviously sent somebody out to buy it for you. Juliet, some glasses and a corkscrew if you would.

(JULIET exits via the kitchen door)

SIMON: You can't rile me today, Donald. The moment is too good to spoil. Any more news – you mentioned July?

DONALD: *(Taking the remaining chair and placing the wine bottle on the table. He is clearly favouring his left hand but* SIMON *seems not to notice).* Juliet has made all the arrangements and has the details. She did some research on these Winsonian bods and they would appear quite genuine. Apparently, they spend their time sifting through the European literature mountain and emerge every three years clutching the name of someone they think worthy of recognition. Obviously, when they finally realised Donald Travers, novelist, Donald James Travers, poet, and D. J. Travers, playwright were all actually one and the same person, then the result was unanimous.

SIMON: Naturally.

DONALD: Stop fawning, dear boy. Ah, here we are.

(JULIET *re-enters with a tray of glasses and a corkscrew)*

SIMON: *(Taking one of the glasses)* Donald was just saying, you've been talking to these Winsonian people. They're coming over in July?

JULIET: Yes. I managed to persuade them that Donald's incontinence made it far too risky for him to travel and –

DONALD: *(Interrupting)* Impudent brat. You are not irreplaceable, you know.

JULIET: Yes I am, don't lie. *(She takes one of the glasses herself and offers the other to* DONALD *who reaches for it with his right hand, winces, then takes it with his left)* What's wrong?

DONALD: Nothing. Simon was asking about the presentation.

JULIET: *(Continuing reluctantly)* I told them that unless they had something specific in mind it would be more convenient if they could come here and they seemed quite amicable. *(Then to DONALD)* You're sure you're okay?

DONALD: Yes! *(Then to SIMON)* Be a good chap and open that.

(SIMON takes the wine bottle and uncorks it expertly. He fills the three glasses)

SIMON: To Donald! May your talent continue to be recognised the world over.

JULIET: Donald!

DONALD: Thank you, thank you.

(They drink. After a few moments there is the sound of a telephone ringing. SIMON produces a mobile 'phone from his jacket pocket)

SIMON: Hello, Simon Courtney – Hi! Yes, okay, no problem – Surely – Of course – Right, fine – Okay – 'Bye – 'Bye.

(As SIMON is talking, JULIET stares at DONALD intently but he refuses to catch her eye)

DONALD: Everything okay?

SIMON: Yes, fine. Unfortunately, I'll have to be going.

(He finishes his wine and places the empty glass on the table) I'll 'phone you in a few days, we need to meet anyway to sort a few things out. Juliet, always a pleasure, I don't know how you manage to put up with him. Goodbye, Donald, and congratulations once again.

JULIET: *(Placing her own glass on the table)* I'll see you out. *(Then to DONALD as SIMON exits via the kitchen)* Don't move! *(She follows SIMON out)* (DONALD *sets his glass down and rises, stretching and rolling his head to relieve a sudden stiffness in his neck.* JULIET *re-enters)*

DONALD: My dear, I –

JULIET: *(Interrupting angrily)* Shut up! Don't lie to me, don't fob me off, and don't try to be funny. I care about you, Donald, and I will not be treated like a well-meaning child. Now, tell me what's wrong.

DONALD: It is nothing, honestly – a cramp, some pins and needles. Honestly, look. *(He reaches for her with his right hand, waggling his fingers in a lecherous gesture. She is unconvinced and raises a hand as if to slap him down)* Come on, stop fussing and let's finish off the wine, it is actually rather good.

(She remains unconvinced but, after a moment, takes up a glass and hands it to him. As she reaches for the

bottle DONALD *suddenly cries out in pain and drops the glass. As* JULIET *rushes to him he is gasping for breath. She helps him into one of the chairs)*

JULIET: *(Panic stricken)* Donald! Oh, God! Donald!

    (She struggles to loosen his collar and belt and holds him upright as he breaths heavily and deeply. It is some time before his breathing returns to normal)

DONALD: *(With difficulty)* You can stop being hysterical now, I am fine.

JULIET: Bullshit! *(Rising)* I'm calling for an ambulance.

DONALD: You will do no such thing.

JULIET: Donald!

DONALD: No! I forbid it.

JULIET: Donald, this is wrong. If you don't at least let me call the doctor out, you – you will never see me naked again.

    (He laughs briefly and she responds despite herself)

    It wasn't meant to be funny. *(Beginning to cry)* This is no time to be funny.

DONALD: I know. I am sorry. Go on, ring the bloody quack.

    (JULIET *exits via the kitchen)*

    (After a deep breath) Oh, Christ.

Early afternoon. A week later. The table and chairs are as before but clear of papers, etc. The sound of typing comes from the shed. The kitchen door is closed, the French windows open. Enter JULIET *and* DOCTOR BRAITHWAITE *via the French windows.*

JULIET: Donald, Doctor Braithwaite is here.

DONALD: *(From the shed)* Tell him I have died.

JULIET: *(Angrily)* Donald! This isn't a joke.

> *(The typing stops and* DONALD *enters from the shed)*

DONALD: Sorry, my dear, sorry. Forgive me, Roger. I was in full flow.

DOCTOR BRAITHWAITE: Ah, the creative muse. Anything interesting?

DONALD: *(Offended)* Of course. How could it not be?

DOCTOR BRAITHWAITE: Forgive me. I meant anything of particular interest to a Philistine like me?

DONALD: *(Appeased)* My autobiography actually.

DOCTOR BRAITHWAITE: Really –

JULIET: *(Interrupting)* Please. Don't start him off –

DONALD: *(Interrupting in turn)* Obnoxious child. Go and fetch some tea. Roger, a refreshing cup?

DOCTOR BRAITHWAITE: If it's not too much trouble. Thank you.

DONALD: Not at all, Roger, not at all. Juliet was just about to make a fresh pot. Off you go, my dear.

JULIET: *(Frowning noticeably. Then with a curtsey)* Yes, master. Right away, master.

DONALD: *(As she exits via the kitchen door)* One cannot get decent servants these days. Ah, you have a look of seriousness all of a sudden.

DOCTOR BRAITHWAITE: This really isn't a laughing matter, Donald.

DONALD: It is my defense mechanism, Roger. For God's sake, if I treat this any other way you might as well shoot me and pack me off the knacker's yard now. I am taking my pills and potions like a good little boy – Christ, Juliet stands over me like bloody Florence Nightingale and checks under my tongue and God knows what else. Do you know what I had for dinner last night? Bloody steamed fish and broccoli!

DOCTOR BRAITHWAITE: Good for you, full of –

DONALD: *(Interrupting)* I know exactly what it's full of and –

JULIET: *(Re-entering via the kitchen with a tray on which are three tea cups and a plate of cake fancies)* Donald!
(She sets the tray down on the table and the three sit; JULIET between DONALD to the right and DOCTOR BRAITHWAITE to the left)
(As they take their seats) Doctor, Darjeeling for you. Donald, hemlock.

DONALD: You see! It is like being in a fucking nursing home.

JULIET: Donald! Forgive him, doctor. He has an IQ of a hundred and fifty-nine, a vocabulary that would startle the average dictionary, and he still finds it amusing to swear broadly whenever we have company.

(*The* DOCTOR *waves a dismissive hand*)

(*Slapping* DONALD's *wrist as he reaches for a cake*) Aaa! Leave those alone.

DONALD: Yes, Matron. (*To the* DOCTOR) You see! (*Then to* JULIET *once more*) You should be more careful, my child, I could always get another research assistant, you know.

JULIET: Of course you could, but they wouldn't put up with you for more than five minutes, and they certainly wouldn't want to have to cuddle up to a lecherous old bugger like you every night!

DONALD: It was not part of the original job description as I recall.

JULIET: Oh, piss off.

DONALD: You must excuse her, Roger. She has an IQ of one hundred and forty-five, a vocabulary which would startle the average scrabble board, and she still finds it amusing to –

JULIET: (*Cutting him short with a laugh*) Drink your tea, Donald.

DONALD: Yes, Matron.

(*They sip their tea in silence for a while. The*

DOCTOR *helps himself to a cake with an apologetic look toward* DONALD. JULIET *makes a show of eating two, one after the other)*

(After a long pause) If this were a scene in a play it would read, 'they sit in silence for a while'.

DOCTOR BRAITHWAITE: Well, if we could be serious for a moment, there are a few questions?

DONALD: *(Magnanimously)* Of course, dear chap, of course.

DOCTOR BRAITHWAITE: Thank you. You say you're taking the pills I prescribed?

DONALD: Oh, yes.

DOCTOR BRAITHWAITE: *(After looking to* JULIET, *who nods in confirmation)* And you're sticking to the diet?

DONALD: Absolutely.

DOCTOR BRAITHWAITE: *(Again he looks to* JULIET, *again the nod)* And you're getting plenty of exercise?

DONALD: Yes, Juliet has me marching up hills and across dales breathing in the air in bloody great lung fulls. *(Then as the* DOCTOR *looks to* JULIET *once more)* Will the two of you please stop this infernal rigmarole, it is like being at Wimbledon.

DOCTOR BRAITHWAITE: Sorry, Donald, sorry. It is important that you follow the regime thoroughly, though.

DONALD: Roger, if you dare tell me that I have been lucky and that I should take what has happened as a warning, I shall write to the British Medical Board and have you struck off immediately for the over-prescribing of cliché and hyperbole.

DOCTOR BRAITHWAITE: *(Laughing)* Wouldn't dream of it. *(Then, helping himself to another cake)* These are rather nice.

DONALD: I will have to take your word for it.

DOCTOR BRAITHWAITE: Home made?

DONALD: Yes, Mister Kipling fashions each one by hand then –

JULIET: *(Interrupting)* Shut up, Donald.

DONALD: My dear girl, the good doctor is attempting to make polite small talk while he tries, vainly, to frame his one remaining question without causing either of us, or himself, embarrassment. *(Enjoying the moment)* Roger?

DOCTOR BRAITHWAITE: *(Clearly embarrassed)* This obviously hasn't dulled your powers of perception at any rate, Donald. Very well. You recall – that is to say – we discussed the matter of – of – well –

DONALD: *(Raising a hand)* Let me put you out of your misery, dear chap. On that score you need have no worries whatsoever. Short of purchasing a chastity belt, Juliet has been the personification of vestal maiden-hood.

JULIET: Abstinence makes the heart grow fonder. That's a pun, Donald.

DONALD: *(Frowning indulgently)* A week is not abstinence, it is bloody torment. If I am to drop dead suddenly I would at least prefer it to happen while I was on the –

JULIET: *(interrupting)* Don't you dare use that phrase about me!

DONALD: – In the loving and tender embrace of the one whom I adore beyond all others. Who –

JULIET: *(Interrupting again)* Shut up, Donald.

DOCTOR BRAITHWAITE: *(Looking at his watch)* Well, if you two will excuse me, I really ought to be getting back.

DONALD: Yes, of course, Roger. Now that you have felt my pulse and eaten me out of house and home, pack up your leeches and be off with you, and let an honest man earn a decent living.

DOCTOR BRAITHWAITE: Ah, yes, the autobiography.

DONALD: Yes. I am thinking of calling it *Look Back In Angst*. You will, of course be mentioned, briefly, as the persecutor of tormented souls. *(Then wagging a finger at* JULIET*)* And as for you – *(He raises a hand as she is about to speak)* I know, 'shut up, Donald'. Very well, make yourself useful, show the good doctor out.

(JULIET *and the* DOCTOR *rise*)

DOCTOR BRAITHWAITE: Goodbye Donald, I'll pop back as soon as I get the results of the tests, but don't hesitate to call in the meantime if you need to.

DONALD: Don't worry, if I break wind without warning, Juliet will ensure that you are the first to know. Goodbye.

DOCTOR BRAITHWAITE: Goodbye, Donald.

DONALD: Goodbye.

(He waits as the DOCTOR *and* JULIET *exit via the French windows and then, making sure that they have gone, he quickly pockets one of the remaining cakes. As* JULIET *re-enters he is standing regarding his finger nails nonchalantly at centre stage)*

JULIET: Put it back.

DONALD: *(Feigning innocence)* I beg your pardon?

JULIET: The cake, Donald. There were four left before I showed the doctor out, now there are only three. You wouldn't have been so stupid as to try and cram it down your throat, so you have obviously stuck it in your pocket to enjoy later.

DONALD: Perhaps Roger –

JULIET: *(Interrupting and getting angry)* Put it back!

DONALD: *(Recognising the tone)* Oh, very well. *(He*

returns the cake to the plate) I suppose I shall have to try and make it through the rest of the afternoon until you serve up another bowl of bread and water for dinner.

JULIET: Actually, I have a treat for you tonight; grilled chicken and vegetables.

DONALD: Including broccoli? (JULIET *nods)* Sounds delicious. Very well, I will continue with my work in the hope that it does not completely drain my strength. Call me if you need a hand to stir the dandelions and nettles. *(He moves toward the shed)*

JULIET: No, it's time for your afternoon constitutional. *(Then, as* DONALD *is about to speak)* Don't argue.

DONALD: *(Resignedly, raising both hands in the air)* Okay, okay, I surrender. Fetch the bath chair and tartan blanket. Go, go, before I faint with anticipation. *(He shoos her off and* JULIET *exits via the French windows.* DONALD *follows, pausing only to pocket one of the cakes as he passes)*

Early morning. Two days later. As before, except that the table is clear. Again, DONALD *can be heard typing from within the shed. The typing stops suddenly.*

DONALD: *(Emerging from the shed)* Shit! *(He is clearly in pain and stretches carefully, arching his back and neck)* Shit! *(He bends forward hands on his thighs)* Shit! *(He stands upright, breathing deeply, arms folded across his chest, his hands pressed against his ribcage)* Juliet! Juliet! *(Then, doubling over again)* Oh, Christ!

(At some point during this the doorbell has rung. Voices are heard briefly from inside the house. Enter JULIET and DOCTOR BRAITHWAITE via the French windows)

JULIET: *(Rushing forward)* Donald! Oh, Jesus! Doctor! *(They help DONALD to one of the chairs)*

DOCTOR BRAITHWAITE: A glass of water, quickly.

(JULIET rushes into the kitchen. The DOCTOR removes a bottle of pills from his bag and empties a couple in to his hand. JULIET returns and hands him a glass of water. He forces DONALD to take the pills and helps him sip the water. It is a while before DONALD is fully recovered)

DONALD: *(Weakly)* You can stop fussing now.

DOCTOR BRAITHWAITE: At the risk of sounding like a cliché, I really was afraid of this.

DONALD: Your concerns are well founded. I assume your presence is not merely well-timed coincidence?

DOCTOR BRAITHWAITE: No, I said I'd come over when the results of the tests arrived. *(He looks to*

JULIET)

JULIET: Are you sure you're okay? Perhaps you should go and lie down for a while?

DONALD: If the two of you are going to treat me like a child I shall take a tantrum and start throwing things around and stamping my foot. For God's sake, Roger, will you please refrain from this mollycoddling bedside manner and get on with it.

DOCTOR BRAITHWAITE: Very well. *(Indicating the chairs and pausing as they all sit)* In lay terms, you've had a mild seizure –

DONALD: *(Interrupting)* Mild! I felt as though somebody was tattooing my chest with a blowtorch!

DOCTOR BRAITHWAITE: Donald, believe me, the initial attack and this just now were mild. The tests they ran at the clinic show that, essentially, what's happening is that the arteries around the heart have weakened, which is putting a strain on your entire system. At times it simply can't cope. The pills I gave you will help. and the diet and exercise are essential, but –

DONALD: *(Interrupting)* But? Are you trying to say this could kill me?

DOCTOR BRAITHWAITE: *(After a moment's hesitation)* Potentially, yes.

JULIET: Oh, God, no.

(They fall silent)

DONALD: *(After a few moments)* 'Potentially' is rather a diplomatic expression, Roger. Not really precise, one might say.

DOCTOR BRAITHWAITE: I'm sorry, both of you, but I can't be more specific. You have to remember that we're talking about the heart here. Every organ is as individual as you are. The attacks you've had may well have killed somebody else on the spot. Another person might not have even been affected by the deterioration yet. I simply can't . . .

DONALD: I am sorry, Roger. Forgive me if I snapped at you. It is not every day one realises one is not as immortal as one thought. *(Then, rising)* If you will excuse me, I think I will have that lie down after all.

JULIET: *(Rising)* Donald . . .

DONALD: Please, I am fine. I just feel suddenly quite tired. *(He exits via the French windows)*

DOCTOR BRAITHWAITE: I'm sorry, I –

JULIET: *(Interrupting)* Doctor Braithwaite, forgive me, but please don't fuck me about. You may have got away with it with Donald while he's in this frame of mind, but he will think it through and then he's going to –

DOCTOR BRAITHWAITE: *(Interrupting in turn)* I know. I simply couldn't throw everything at him at once. You have to remember I've known Donald for nearly twenty-five years, he's a friend as well as a patient.

JULIET: *(After a moment)* So. Deep breath. How long?

DOCTOR BRAITHWAITE: Six months, a year. I really can't be more accurate.

JULIET: *(After several moments digesting the news in which she wipes away tears with both hands but remains otherwise calm)* I don't want him to know. *(Then, as the DOCTOR is about to interrupt)* No! I'm not having him sitting around waiting to die. For Christ's sake, Doctor, can you imagine what it would do to him? Let him live his life as fully as he can. Let him get on with his work as normal, let him pinch the odd cream cake when he thinks no one is looking, let him just be Donald. If – when – it happens, I assume it will be quite sudden? *(The DOCTOR nods his head)* And quick? *(He nods again)* Okay – then, he's not to know. Please.

DOCTOR BRAITHWAITE: *(After several moment's consideration)* If he asks me directly, if he specifically puts the question of time to me, I will have to inform him. You must appreciate that. (JULIET *nods*) Very well, unless he asks,

I'll say nothing.

JULIET: Thank you.

DOCTOR BRAITHWAITE: And what about you? How will you manage, would you like me to send a nurse round? I can make all the arrangements if you –

JULIET: *(Interrupting)* No, I'll cope. I think it would be easier if there were just Donald and me.

DOCTOR BRAITHWAITE: You're sure?

JULIET: Yes. Thank you, anyway.

As a silence falls SIMON *enters stage left)*

SIMON: There you are. I think your doorbell must be broken – pressed the damn thing for ages. Been in New York for a few days, came as soon as I got your message. How is he?

JULIET: *(Momentarily flustered)* He's having a rest at the moment. Do you know Doctor Braithwaite?

SIMON: No, no, I don't believe we've met. Simon Courtney, Donald's agent. *(Then as the two shake hands)* How do you do?

JULIET: *(Recovering her composure)* The Doctor was just saying that if Donald maintains his diet and keeps taking his prescription he should have everything under control.

SIMON: Oh, that is good news. Wouldn't want to lose the old bugger just yet, eh?

DOCTOR BRAITHWAITE: No, quite. *(He makes a show of*

examining his watch) Well, if the two of you will
excuse me, I must be off.

JULIET: Yes, of course.

SIMON: Fine. Nice to have met you, Doctor. Goodbye.

DOCTOR BRAITHWAITE: Goodbye. I'll see myself out.
(He gathers his things together) Goodbye.

JULIET: Goodbye – and thank you.
(The DOCTOR exits via the French windows)

SIMON: Donald's quack, eh? Seems like a nice chap.

JULIET: He is. Knows exactly what's best for Donald.
Please, Simon, forgive me, take a seat.

SIMON: *(Sitting)* Thank you. You say Donald is having a
lie down. Not like him, not at this time of day.
You sure everything is okay?

JULIET: No, actually he had another attack. A mild one,
nothing serious. He just needs to take things a
bit easier, that's all. You know what Donald's
like, won't be told until it's – until you
eventually have to hit him over the head with a
hammer, or something . . . *(She finishes lamely
and turns away, a hand to her brow)*

SIMON: *(Rising)* Hey, you okay?

JULIET: *(Recovering)* Yes, sorry, I'm fine. The last few
days have just been a bit of a trauma, to say the
least. I'm fine, honestly.

SIMON: You sure? Here, have a seat. *(She sits)* So, the old
sod's not too good, eh?

JULIET: No, he'll be fine. Just needs to follow doctor's orders and cut out the wild orgies and drunken binges.

SIMON: *(Smiling indulgently)* And you'll be playing the ministering angel, I suppose?

JULIET: Who else? You know Donald's always had a thing for women in nurse's uniform. I like to indulge him every so often. Keeps him young.

SIMON: *(Laughing)* Well, if you're sure everything will be okay?

JULIET: Honestly, we'll be fine. The autobiography is coming along really well.

SIMON: I think that's called changing the subject – but, since you mention it . . .

JULIET: He's been wading through mountains of old letters and photo albums and stuff. Half the stories I've heard before but some of the anecdotes from his time at university and the early days are hysterical. Some of the people he mentions are probably going to sue him for every penny he's got.

SIMON: Sounds great. How's the editing going?

JULIET: Oh, the usual. I make corrections or suggest alterations, he calls me an interfering little busybody and changes them back, then the next draft comes through with most of the amendments made as if they're all his idea, and he calls me more names for not making the changes in the first place.

SIMON: Yes, that sounds like Donald. *(They both laugh, briefly, then fall silent)*

JULIET: *(Heavily)* Simon, I don't know what's the matter with me today. I haven't even offered you a cup of tea or anything. *(She rises)*

SIMON: No, please I'm fine. Anyway, if the old boy's not up and about I'd probably be best getting off and leaving you to it. *(He rises)*

JULIET: *(Relieved but not showing it)* You're sure?

SIMON: Yes, best be going. Tell Donald I called in and ask him to ring me at the office tomorrow if he thinks on, we need to chat anyway.

JULIET: Okay.

SIMON: When do you think the 'script will be ready?

JULIET: Should have the draft ready in a couple of months, three maybe. To be honest, it depends on how much he wants to put in it, how many people he wants to upset, and which sacred cows he wants to have a go at.

SIMON: Now I really can't wait. Might have to have our legal advisors on stand-by though from the sound of it.

(Again they laugh briefly but the strain is beginning to show)

JULIET: Well, drive safely. I'll let Donald know you

popped in, I'm sure he'll be straight on the 'phone.

SIMON: Fine. Well, take care. I'll go back out this way. See you again soon. 'Bye.

JULIET: *(As he exits stage left)* 'Bye. 'Bye.

> *(She stands quite still for a moment then, finally, bursts into tears before collapsing into one of the chairs, her head in her hands, and sobbing unrestrainedly)*

An hour or so later. JULIET is asleep at the table, her head resting on her folded arms. Enter DONALD via the kitchen door. He looks tired and somewhat disheveled. Seeing JULIET he runs a hand through his hair and makes an attempt at straightening his collar and waistband. He approaches JULIET and stands over her for several moments simply watching her. As if suddenly sensing his presence she wakes with a start.

DONALD: Okay, only me. You had fallen asleep.

JULIET: Sorry, I –

DONALD: *(Interrupting)* No, I think we both needed it. I suppose Roger shot straight off?

JULIET: Yes, yes. He left right after you went to bed. *(Then hurriedly)* Simon called in, he's been in New York. He wanted to know when the ego trip would be finished. Oh, and can you ring him tomorrow, he wants to gossip about how wonderful the Big Apple is again.

DONALD: Bless him, he does play the Englishman abroad in the big city to perfection.

JULIET: You tease him too much. He's very sensitive.

DONALD: Are you being euphemistic, child?

JULIET: Stop showing your age, you sound like an old bigot.

DONALD: My dear girl, I have moved in the grandest of literary circles for the past thirty years and have met individuals of every conceivable temperament and predilection. I am the most tolerant, understanding, and non-judgemental of people. If Simon happens to have a limp handshake, that is entirely his business.

JULIET: What a cliché!

DONALD: It was meant to be, my dear, we call it being sardonic. A grown up trait you may one day attain, if you practice hard enough.

JULIET: You're feeling better then.

DONALD: Yes, sorry. How are you, you look bloody awful.

JULIET: Thank you, Donald, as sweet as ever.

DONALD: A natural talent which comes with experience. *(Then after a moment)* So, now that we have had the idle chit-chat and you think all is well, let us be serious for a moment. What did Roger have to say that he could not bring himself to tell me directly, hm?

JULIET: *(Determinedly)* Nothing that he hadn't already said. Stick to the diet, take your pills like a good little boy, and get plenty of gentle exercise. He particularly stressed the word 'gentle'.

DONALD: *(Shaking his head)* I am sure he did, in his own inimitable way. And then?

JULIET: And then he left. Donald, please don't try to make this in to a bigger issue than needs be. I'm worried enough about you as it is, don't do this to me, please.

(There is a silence between them for several seconds)

DONALD: Very well, we will let it drop for the moment. Was the phrase 'ego trip' Simon's, or were you paraphrasing?

JULIET: *(Smiling in relief)* Your thought processes never cease to amaze me! One minute we're talking about the state of your health, and the next about some casual remark.

DONALD: Both of equal importance to me in their own way.

JULIET: Donald! *(Then, laughing)* Okay, I was being flippant, but what makes you think anyone will be the remotest bit interested in the ramblings of an old phony like you?

DONALD: My dear child, the response from those to whom I have mentioned it has been universal anticipation. There are so many people now wondering if they will be mentioned, and what I will say of them, that they have probably already placed an advance order. I anticipate it will be the number one best-seller for some considerable time when it is published.

JULIET: You see this as the ultimate Kiss and Tell story then?

DONALD: More Bliss and Hell, I think. The good, the bad, and the occasionally very ugly.

JULIET: And which of those am I?

DONALD: All three, to varying degrees, dependent upon your mood.

JULIET: Thank you. Perhaps I should ring the tabloids now and give them my version. How you drugged and seduced me, and keep me locked in a dark and damp dungeon with only the occasional bowl of gruel.

DONALD: The drugs you brought with you. The seduction was mutual. I have a cellar, amply stocked and well ventilated, not a dungeon. I am a superb cook, as you well know, and it is I who has had to suffer bowls of gruel lately, not you.

JULIET: I was being sarcastic, Donald. A juvenile trait which you will long have forgotten and –

DONALD: *(Interrupting)* Oh, shut up and give me a hug.

(They hold each other close and there is a mutual relief in the embrace. Then JULIET *pulls away suddenly)*

JULIET: Donald!

DONALD: *(Innocently)* What?

JULIET: Behave yourself.

DONALD: My dear girl, the day you cease to have this effect on me is the day you can call the undertaker.

JULIET: Not funny, Donald.

DONALD: I was not joking. Still, seems a shame to waste it, now it has risen to the occasion, so to speak.

JULIET: You know what Doctor Braithwaite said.

DONALD: Yes, he told you to be gentle with me. I promise to let you do all the work.

JULIET: Nothing new there, then.

DONALD: Am I to take that as a yes, hm?

JULIET: *(Shaking her head and laughing)* Sometimes . . .

(He slips an arm around her waist and they exit via the French windows)

ACT TWO

Mid-afternoon. Early summer about two months later. The kitchen door and window and the French windows are all open. The shed door and windows are closed. The umbrella has been set to the table and stands open, shading JULIET who *sits at one of the chairs, pen in hand, reading a sheet from a stack of papers before her. Glasses, a jug of orange juice, and cans of soft drinks are set out on the table.*

JULIET: Sometimes, Donald, you go too far. *(She draws a line through a section of the text and continues reading)*

DONALD: *(Entering via the kitchen with a large glass full of ice cubes which he sets down beside the drinks)* How goes it, my precious? Are you swept away by the dazzling images of the literary world?

JULIET: *(Rising)* There is no way you'll get away with this.

DONALD: Which?

JULIET: *(Handing him the sheet and indicating the passage she has crossed out)* This!

DONALD: *(After reading for a moment)* Perfectly true, ask anyone.

JULIET: Proof, Donald?

DONALD: I am merely stating facts, my love. Well known facts to which he has readily admitted.

JULIET: In writing? On tape, or video?

DONALD: Of course not. In private and while under the influence of several bottles of a rather superior Burgundy; but they are still facts.

JULIET: Gossip, hearsay, and undoubtedly libellous.

DONALD: Nonsense. Everyone knows it to be true.

JULIET: Would they be willing to stand up in court and say so?

DONALD: *(After a moment's thought)* No, perhaps not. I suppose you can tone it down a bit.

JULIET: *(Resuming her seat)* Thank you.

DONALD: Not too much though, it is still fundamentally true, despite your lack of conviction and unwillingness to support me.

JULIET: Don't sulk. *(Then, as he is about to speak)* Pour me some Coke. *(Again, as he is about to speak)* Shut up.

(Defeated, he does as he is told. She takes the proffered glass without looking up or thanking him. After a moment he wanders off toward the shed but, drawing near, changes his mind and simply stands idly gazing off into the distance)

DONALD: *(After a while)* Cabbage patch is coming along nicely.

JULIET: Don't be feeble, Donald, we don't have a cabbage patch. Petulance doesn't become you.

DONALD: Of course it does, I am an artist of the highest

order with a temperament to match. I have every right to run the emotive gauntlet as I see fit, whenever the mood takes me. Right now, the mood takes me. As one who supposedly dotes on me, I would have expected you to understand without the need of explanation. *(He finishes with a sniff and turns away once more)*

JULIET: *(Putting the papers aside resignedly)* Right. Okay. For the sixth thousandth time, I apologise.

DONALD: And for the sixth thousandth time, I accept.

JULIET: Thank you.

DONALD: But you still should not have done it.

JULIET: Oh, for Christ's sake, can we stop this! She's your daughter, Donald, your only child. She has a right to know.

DONALD: She does not have a right to know anything which I expressly choose not to tell her! You do not have the right to tell her anything!

JULIET: Thank you, Donald.

DONALD: Oh, Juliet, damn it! I love you, and I love Susan. You are the only two people on the entire planet I can actually say that about. It is bad enough that you have to go through this with me, do you think I would willingly have it inflicted on Susan as well?

JULIET: *(Rising)* Donald, I'm really sorry. I just . . .

DONALD: I know, I know. Come here and – shit!

JULIET: *(Panicking)* Donald!

DONALD: Relax, relax, this is just emotional tension. Pour me a glass of that orange juice to cool my fevered brow.

JULIET: *(Doing so)* Here. Are you going to be all right?

DONALD: *(Finishing the drink)* Yes, yes, stop fussing. What time do they arrive?

JULIET: *(Glancing at her watch)* Any minute now.

DONALD: Good, good. I wonder how she got on with that audition? I bumped into the director in the bar of the National when I was last in London for the new Stoppard. Had a brief word with him, so it should have been a formality –

JULIET: *(Interrupting)* Donald, you didn't! She'll have your balls for conkers if she finds out.

DONALD: Vulgarity is not one of your most endearing traits.

JULIET: Oh, I thought you liked it when I talked dirty?

DONALD: You know exactly what I mean, besides which, it was Tony who raised the matter, I merely agreed that Susan was supremely talented and would be ideal for the part. Okay?

JULIET: So long as that's all it was, you know what will happen – *(She is interrupted by the doorbell ringing)* That'll be them now. I'll get it.

(She exits via the French windows)

(DONALD stands waiting impatiently as voices are

heard from inside the house. After a few moments
JULIET, SUSAN, *and* ASLAN *enter via the French
windows)*

DONALD: Susan, darling, wonderful to see you again.
(They embrace warmly) Bas, my boy. *(They shake
hands heartily)* Please, sit, sit. Have you eaten,
we prepared some picnicky titbits just in case?
Still vegetarians the two of you? Juliet?
*(He collects the papers together and puts them to one
side as Juliet makes for the kitchen)*

SUSAN: *(As the three take seats at the table)* Cut the caring
host crap, you old fart, it won't work. Just get to
the point and tell me how you are.

DONALD: Ah, you have obviously been spending some
time with your dear mother again. That
attitude of hers is contagious you know, if you
are not careful.

SUSAN: I haven't seen Katherine since Easter; don't try
to change the subject. Jules said this was
serious and that you were behaving in your
usual contemptuous manner.

DONALD: Ah, dear Juliet, she does tend to overstate
things and worry so.
*(JULIET re-enters carrying a tray stacked with
various savory snacks and so on)*

JULIET: *(Setting the tray on the table and taking the
remaining seat)* Here we are.

DONALD: Ah, I was just saying how well you are nurturing me in my decline into senility.

JULIET: I heard you, you toad.

DONALD: Ah.

ASLAN: We really were quite concerned when we heard, Donald, we would have come sooner only –

DONALD: *(Interrupting)* Nonsense. You are both extremely busy and you are here now, that –

SUSAN: *(Interrupting in turn)* And still waiting to hear the details from the horse's mouth – or perhaps the orifice at the other end, if you insist on talking fatuous horseshit.

DONALD: *(Wagging a finger between* JULIET *and* SUSAN*)* There is no chance that the two of you are twins separated at birth, is there?

SUSAN: I shall slap you in a minute.

DONALD: *(Resignedly)* Okay, okay. I have a weakening of the arteries around the heart which is putting pressure on my entire system and at times it cannot cope. I have had a series of mild seizures, the last eight days ago. The term 'mild' is my doctor's so you can see there is nothing to worry about. I have pills and potions enough to stock a branch of Boots, and nursey here has me eating rabbit food and strolling the length and breadth of the countryside. I could not be better. Okay?

SUSAN: I just wanted to have you look me in the eye when you said it.

DONALD: Which one?

SUSAN: *(To* JULIET) I don't know how you put up with him.

JULIET: Pity plays a large part.

DONALD: If the two of you are going to start your witless double act I shall have Bas accompany me to the nearest pub for two large lemonades on the rocks and leave you to it.

JULIET: He appears to be implying we gang up on him, Sue.

DONALD: Stop it, you brat. Are these seaweed parcels and nutty whatnots actually edible or do we merely sit and stare at them until they turn into useful garden compost?

ASLAN: *(As he and the others help themselves)* I don't suppose your diet allows for too many spices or I could give you some really nice recipes.

DONALD: Alas, control of the shopping trolley has been wrestled from my grip. One is reduced to sitting in the toddler's seat and grasping despairingly at items as we whiz down the aisles.

SUSAN: If you're attempting to play the sympathy vote, it won't work. Jules has our full support. Whatever she feels is best is fine by me.

DONALD: So much for family unity.

JULIET: Sue and I seem to be very united, Donald.

DONALD: In that you both seek to take advantage of my generous nature and my unwillingness to crush you beneath the full weight of my wit and – *(He is interrupted by their collective laughter)*

(Then, shaking his head as it dies down) I despair. *(Rallying)* As for you, my boy, stand your ground before it is too later. If you allow her too much leeway now you will live to regret it, I warn you.

ASLAN: I'll take my chances.

JULIET: *(After they have fallen silent for a moment)* Donald mentioned that you'd been for an audition, Sue.

DONALD: *(After frowning at* JULIET *knowingly)* Yes, how did you get on, my darling?

SUSAN: As if you didn't know. I got the part. *(To* JULIET*)* Eliza in Pygmalion.

(Then, pointedly to DONALD*)* Tony had already made up his mind.

DONALD: I know! I know! I said as much to Juliet. I merely agreed with him that you were ideal for the part. Anyone would think one had offered him money, or revealed some candid photographs of him by way of blackmail – though there are actually enough of those around already. You got the role on natural merit; forgive me for playing the proud father, one simply wanted to know if you had been successful, and there he was next to me at the bar.

JULIET: For once I think he may be telling the truth.

SUSAN: Okay, I'm sorry, forgive me.

DONALD: *(Magnanimously)* Think nothing of it. Send us two complementary box tickets for the first night and we will say no more. When do you open?

SUSAN: Not for a month or so yet.

DONALD: And you, my boy, anything on the horizon? I thought you were excellent in the Stoppard, by the way.

Aslan: Thank you. I have a couple of potential TV commercials lined up, and there's a new series about the Mounbattens in India coming up on the BBC, which has several interesting parts on offer.

DONALD: Excellent. It is good to know that the fees will be readily available if I ever need to retire to one of those rest homes for the chronically frail and bewildered which Juliet keeps pointing out to me in various magazines advertisements.

JULIET: *(As they all laugh)* Always best to be prepared, Donald.

SUSAN: So, you old fart, tell us all about this award you're getting, Jules tells us you've been insufferably conceited since you found out.

DONALD: I refuse to rise to your childish goading. If you persist I shall merely ignore you with the contempt you deserve.

SUSAN: Very well. *(To* JULIET *and* ASLAN) Shall we go inside?

(All three rise)

DONALD: Brats! Very well, far be it from me to gloat, but since you insist. *(They resume their seats)* The Winsonian Society of Philadelphia, a noble institution of international renown, has selected me as the recipient of its prestigious triennial award for services to world literature and global peace and understanding.

SUSAN: I'm impressed. What did you do to deserve it, may one ask?

DONALD: The award is presented for a body of work over the years which best encapsulates their worthy philosophy.

ASLAN: And what did you do to deserve it, may one ask?

DONALD: *(As the others laugh)* You are obviously spending far too much time with my daughter. Perhaps you should film on location more often? *(They all laugh)*

ASLAN: I'll take my chances.

SUSAN: So, when's the big day?

DONALD: Next week. Tuesday, I believe. *(He looks to* JULIET *who nods)* They insist on making a bloody big fuss as usual and presenting me with what sounds like an absolutely horrendous trophy of some sort.

JULIET: Two doves in a laurel wreath.

SUSAN: *(Laughing)* Jesus!

DONALD: See!

JULIET: Please, don't encourage him.

SUSAN: Sorry.

DONALD: You know what the Americans are like, no subtlety. *(Then, quickly)* Present company excepted, of course.

JULIET: Thank you.

ASLAN: I believe there's a cash award as well.

DONALD: Yes, I have insisted they make it payable in sterling, of course. Juliet has done the sums and it is a not inconsiderable amount, I have to admit.

JULIET: He has no problems taking their money, you'll notice.

DONALD: Meaning?

SUSAN: *(Taking a bit of one of the cakes from the tray)* Is there any lemon in this?

JULIET: *(Somewhat confused)* No, why?

SUSAN: I suddenly got a sense of something bitter.

DONALD: Your mother's traits are really taking a firmer hold than you think, my dear.

SUSAN: Really? She always says I'm just like you.

JULIET: Oh, please, let's not start on this again.

DONALD: I am not starting anything.

SUSAN: Of course you are. Go on then, get it off your chest. Again.

DONALD: I have no idea what you might mean.

SUSAN: Bullshit, you know very well what I mean, this continuous need to snipe every time her name is mentioned.

DONALD: Snipe! The woman left me for a short-arsed troglodyte with a curly-perm and bad aftershave. While I was holed up in some flea pit of a hotel re-writing scenes of the film she was in at the director's insistence, she was fucking the bloody director in another hotel across the road. And you sense a little bitterness!

JULIET: Donald, calm down.

SUSAN: Okay, I'm sorry, I'm sorry. It's obviously still a painful subject, but you can't go on opening up old wounds like this. Blaming her every five minutes isn't going to change anything, is it?

DONALD: What? You think I blame Katherine? I loved your mother dearly and have always attempted to be as civil about her as the circumstances allow. Please do not take my pleasure at ribbing you as criticism of her, it is not. Katherine is an individual with every right to do as she wished and, while it is something I still do not understand, and while it may have hurt immensely, it was, when all is said and done, her choice to make. I wish she had discussed it civilly instead of getting involved in such sordid antics but, as I say, that was her choice and her right.

SUSAN: But the same didn't apply to Richard, obviously.

DONALD: That obnoxious little tomcat should be filleted and fried in oil.

ASLAN: Being a vegetarian, fried fillet of tomcat isn't something I could see myself preparing, but if it's something you'd specifically like next time you visit . . .

(The tension is broken and they are all able to laugh)

DONALD: Thank you, my boy, for putting things in their correct perspective. *(Then, to SUSAN)* Take note, my love, you could learn a lot if you have the sense not to lose him.

SUSAN: I'll do my best to hang on to him, father, dearest. Thank you for sharing your wisdom.

JULIET: *(After a moment)* Donald, while I've heard nearly every story you've ever had to tell at least a dozen times and, while most of them weren't the least bit entertaining the first time –

DONALD: *(Interrupting archly)* Careful, my dear, I have warned you, do not be carried away by the thought that there is safety in numbers.

JULIET: *(Smiling indulgently)* There *is* one story while we seem to be on the subject . . .

DONALD: Yes?

JULIET: Did you really beat up this Richard person?

SUSAN: Did he ever.

ASLAN: Jesus!

DONALD: Should that not be Mohammed, my boy?

JULIET: Donald!

DONALD: What? You have read the episode, it is all there in black and white.

SUSAN: What's he rambling about now?

JULIET: Donald has been compiling his autobiography for the last few months. I'm working my way through the final draft now. Editing shouldn't take too long, we've been amending as we go anyway, and –

SUSAN: *(Interrupting)* My God! I want to see a copy before it goes anywhere near your publishers.

DONALD: Certainly not! The very impudence of it!

JULIET: Relax. I've managed to remove the blatantly opinionated and offensive passages; you can imagine how many of those there were! Just think of it as the bitter memoirs of one who –

DONALD: Enough, the two of you. This will be the crowning glory of my career, littered with revealing personal anecdotes, historical counterpoints, and incidental titbits on the great and not so good.

ASLAN: Including the punch-up with this Richard chap?

DONALD: Of course.

ASLAN: *(After a moment)* So what happened?

SUSAN: *(To DONALD)* Do you want to do this or shall I keep it as simple and near to the facts as possible?

ASLAN: What, you were there?

DONALD: She certainly was, and a vital role she played in the events, it has to be said.

ASLAN: *(To SUSAN)* You never mentioned any of this.

SUSAN: I was fourteen years old; it isn't the most dignified episode in my brief but eventful life.

ASLAN: So, since I seem to be the only one who is ignorant of the facts, is one of you going to tell me what happened?

DONALD: Well, having found out about it, I confronted them in the hotel restaurant and –

SUSAN: *(Interrupting)* And there was an almighty scene. Mother broke down in a flood of tears and admitted everything –

DONALD: *(Interrupting)* One of her better performances,

I thought.

SUSAN: Shut up! *(Then continuing)* Mother was obviously nearly hysterical. His majesty here was ranting and raving like a demented –

DONALD: *(Interrupting again)* I have never either ranted or raved in my life. You said you would be concise and to the point. I merely informed them both of exactly what I thought of them, where they could both go, and what they could do when they got there. Continue.

SUSAN: Thank you. I had been swimming in our hotel pool and was on my way back to my room when the desk clerk came running up to inform me that my father had just stormed out heading for the hotel across the road, ranting and raving, his words, and with a face like thunder. I didn't know what the hell was going on but I took off across the road after him –

DONALD: *(Interrupting once more)* Still in her swim suit.

SUSAN: I won't tell you again.

(DONALD *grins broadly and spreads his arms wide)* I caught up with him in the restaurant; the way he was shouting it wasn't too difficult to trace him, and just as I arrived Richard panicked and made a lunge, and Rocky Travers here decked him then proceeded to try and wrap one of the chairs around his neck.

ASLAN: And you . . .?

DONALD: If I may, purely to spare you the embarrassment of having to relate your own act of gratuitous violence?

(SUSAN *nods*)

My darling daughter arrived just as one of The Dick's minions, whom I had not noticed, was sneaking up behind me . . . (*He pauses for effect, savoring the moment and* SUSAN's *obvious discomfort*)

ASLAN: And?

DONALD: And then, with no thought for her own safety, acting without hesitation –

SUSAN: (*Interrupting*) Get on with it, you vindictive bastard.

DONALD: She crowned him with a handy champagne bottle.

ASLAN: No!

DONALD: Oh, it was empty.

SUSAN: (*As the others laugh*) Stop it!

DONALD: Yes, amid the anguish of the recollection, that one moment still fills me with an undeniable glow and burgeoning paternal pride.

SUSAN: Stop it!

DONALD: Oh, come on, the sight of The Dick protruding through tattered raffia-work and his little arse-wiper flat out and gurgling inanely –

(They all, including SUSAN, laugh)

SUSAN: *(After a moment)* Okay, okay, but will you please stop calling him The Dick. It –

ASLAN: *(Interrupting)* No, go on, what happened then?

DONALD: Then the local sheriff and his deputies arrived and carted us all off to the county jail and –

ASLAN: *(Interrupting)* No!

DONALD: Afraid so, my boy. You are living with a hardened criminal who –

SUSAN: *(Interrupting)* All right, enough! Jules, help!

JULIET: Whoa, leave me out of this one, with your reputations the last thing I want to do is get caught up in a family feud.

SUSAN: Bitch!

JULIET: *(Laughing)* Okay, okay. About six hours ago someone mentioned going to the pub. Under the circumstances, Donald, I am willing to allow you one pint of shandy – if you promise to behave.

DONALD: With such a tempting bribe, you have my word of honour, my dear. Of course, it may well be best if we do not order champagne, just in case . . .

SUSAN: I refuse to be drawn any further. I need an alcoholic haze to blot out the memories, make sure you bring your wallet.

DONALD: Ah, your mother's very – (SUSAN *glares at him*) Sorry. Lead on.

(*They all rise and* ASLAN *and* SUSAN *lead the way exiting via the French windows.* DONALD *and* JULIET *follow close behind.* JULIET *closes the windows behind her*)

The following week. Mid-afternoon. The patio is deserted. The table and chairs are laid out as before, the table is clear. The kitchen door is closed the French windows ajar. The door to the shed opens and DONALD *leans out, scanning the patio and straining to hear any noise from within. Disappointed, he withdraws and closes the door. About ten seconds later he repeats the action and again withdraws. Another ten seconds pass and he appears again. As he does so* JULIET *enters via the French windows accompanied by* ROBIN BENJAMIN *and* HOWARD McPHERSONN. *The three are talking amongst themselves and do not notice* DONALD's *hasty withdrawal.*

JULIET: Ah, he must still be working. (*Then loudly*) Donald. Donald, our guests have arrived.

DONALD: (*Entering from the shed*) Forgive me, forgive me, I was miles away. Once one gets into one's work one loses all track of time.

JULIET: Let me make some introductions. Donald Travers. Robin Benjamin, Secretary of the Winsonian Society of Philadelphia –

DONALD: *(Aside, as he moves toward* HOWARD *with his hand outstretched)* Just as I thought, crusty old codger.

JULIET: And Howard McPhersonn, the Society's Director.

DONALD: *(Realising his mistake but continuing without breaking stride)* Mr McPhersonn. *(They shake hands)*

MR McPHERSONN: That's McPhersonn with two Ns; as in the original Scottish spelling of the fifteenth century.

DONALD: Really? You must tell me all about it sometime. Ms Benjamin, delighted. *(They shake hands in turn)* Please, take a seat. *(Then, as they all sit)* You must have had a long journey, it really is most kind of you to come all this way.

MR McPHERSONN: Not at all, not at all, I like to get over here as often as I can. I've been working on my family tree you know, I'm back to 1432, sixty years before Christopher Columbus landed in North America –

DONALD: *(Interrupting)* Really? You must tell me all about it sometime. And you, Ms Benjamin –

MS BENJAMIN: *(Interrupting)* Please, call me Robin.

DONALD: Robin. You have visited before?

MS BENJAMIN: No, my first time here, actually. A pity really as we only flew in yesterday and we fly on to Prague tomorrow, so I won't really have any time to see anything.

DONALD: What a shame. Prague, you say?

MR McPHERSONN: Yes, we're in the process of opening our first residential school outside of the United States. The Society is most keen to encourage potential writing talent in Eastern Europe, now that freedom of speech is no longer an alien concept there.

MS BENJAMIN: *(Keenly and before* DONALD *can respond)* Yes, we hope to develop several centres across Europe eventually. Small self-contained establishments, fully staffed, with guest lecturers who share our philosophy and belief in the nurturing and development of creativity.

DONALD: Good God!

MR McPHERSONN: *(Misinterpreting)* Indeed. Truly awe inspiring, isn't it.

DONALD: *(Confounded)* I really do not know what to say.

JULIET: *(Quickly, sensing how things could develop)* Donald, perhaps you'd like to show our guests your study, then we could step indoors for drinks, if that would be acceptable?

MR McPHERSONN: Certainly, it would be a pleasure indeed to see the inner sanctum of such a worthy scribe.

DONALD: *(Struggling to keep a benign smile on his face as he gestures toward the shed)* Please, after you. *(As the two move off he turns to JULIET and makes a gesture as if running a blade across his throat, tongue lolling and eyes bulging)*

(JULIET *responds with a warning look and points a finger at him in a gesture he readily recognises. Shaking his head, he follows them into the shed and voices can be heard briefly. After a few moments a telephone rings inside the house and JULIET rushes to answer it, exiting via the French windows)*

MR McPHERSONN: *(As they re-emerge)* Amazing, heating, electric lighting, a refrigerator, truly amazing.

DONALD: Thank you; I am toying with the idea of satellite television for those idle moments between chapters.

MR McPHERSONN: Really? – Ah, your English sense of humour. I did notice though that you still use a typewriter and not a PC.

DONALD: *(Comprehending after a moment)* Oh, a computer. Yes, I am, alas, set in my ways. It was a great achievement, I felt, moving on from quill and ink some years ago.

MR McPHERSONN: I wouldn't be without mine, I have to admit; an invaluable tool and so versatile once you grasp the basics. I take my iPad with me everywhere –

JULIET: *(Re-entering via the French windows and saving* DONALD *from further technological confusion)* Excuse me. Donald, Simon's on the 'phone. I did tell him you were busy, but you know what he's like.

DONALD: Indeed. *(Then, to* MS BENJAMIN *and* MR McPHERSONN*)* My agent. If you would excuse me for a moment?

MS BENJAMIN: Of course.

MR McPHERSONN: By all means.

(DONALD *exits via the French windows)*

JULIET: What do you make of Donald's little cubby-hole?

MR McPHERSONN: I was just saying how remarkable it was, a neat twist on the writer's garret of old.

JULIET: I think Donald would actually feel quite at home in a garret, so long as he had his essential comforts.

MS BENJAMIN: Yes, I'm sure. *(Then, archly)* And how long have you been with him?

JULIET: *(After pursing her lips for a moment)* I started off as his research assistant for a novel he was working on about four years ago. He'd never used one before, but after he gave a series of lectures at the university I was attending I pestered him and pestered him until he gave in.

MS BENJAMIN: And after the novel?

JULIET: I stayed on.

MS BENJAMIN: As his assistant?

JULIET: Assistant, secretary, housemaid, lover. The role developed with time.

MR McPHERSONN: *(With as sudden coughing fit)* And originally you are from – I sense a familiar accent, do I not?

JULIET: Yes, I'm from Baltimore originally, although I grew up in Boston. My mother and I moved to Richmond when my parents divorced.

DONALD: *(Aside as he re-enters)* My God, I have stumbled into an audition for Gone with the Wind.

MR McPHERSONN: And then you came to England to study?

JULIET: Yes. *(Then as DONALD approaches)* Ah, Donald, everything okay?

DONALD: Yes, fine, you know what Simon is like, everything is a crisis.

MS BENJAMIN: Nothing serious?

DONALD: No, no. Juliet has been entertaining you I hope.

MS BENJAMIN: Oh, yes, she's been most informative.

MR McPHERSONN: *(Quickly)* If I may make so bold, could I suggest we move indoors to make the presentation and take a few photographs.

DONALD: Photographs?

MR MCPHERSONN: Yes, nothing too formal, but we obviously like to report events such as this in our journal and one or two of the more literary publications in the United States are always keen to have the details. Perhaps you could advise us on any of your British publications which might be equally as interested?

DONALD: Of course, of course, please, lead on.

> (*Then, catching JULIET by the arm as the others exit via the French windows*) They *have* literary publications in America?

JULIET: (*Pushing him ahead of her*) You *will* behave.

DONALD: (*As they follow on*) Yes, my sweet. Of course, anything you say, you only have to . . .

About two hours later. JULIET stands in the middle of the patio with her back to the house. She is drinking the remaining wine straight from the bottle. She is slightly tipsy and clearly deep in thought.

DONALD: (*As he enters via the kitchen door*) Christ, I thought they were never going.

JULIET: Bastard!

DONALD: I beg your pardon? Have we been having an argument while I was not here?

JULIET: Don't try to be clever, it won't work.

DONALD: One does not have to try, as you well know. Come on, please, tell me what the problem is.

JULIET: Where would you like me to start?

DONALD: The beginning is often the most appropriate point.

JULIET: You were flirting with her.

DONALD: I was not.

JULIET: You were; incorrigibly, and right in front of me.

DONALD: No, she was flirting, I was simply being polite.

JULIET: Bastard!

DONALD: Juliet, for God's sake, be sensible. Is it really me to behave in such a way? I may be a lot of things, but an insensitive arsehole is not one of them.

JULIET: That would depend on who you asked.

DONALD: Can we stop this?

JULIET: *(Taking a deep breath)* Okay, she grated on me and I may be shifting the blame from her to you in absentia, but what was all that other crap about?

DONALD: Which particular dollop are you referring to specifically?

JULIET: All that about nurturing fledgling talent and unlocking the great untapped store of literary creativeness.

DONALD: Mr McPhersonn, with two n's, and Ms

Benjamin, presumably with one n, were speaking in a language which they appear to have created for their own use. Once one grasped the thrust of what they were trying to say it was fairly simple, if somewhat tortuous of Mother English, to participate in a comparatively sensible conversation.

JULIET: What?

DONALD: They were talking bollocks, I simply joined in.

JULIET: You agreed with them!

DONALD: Once one had managed to translate what they were getting at, it actually sounded fairly commendable. Indulgent, patronising, and pompous to the point of arrogance, to be sure, but there was a germ of worthiness at the core, I must admit.

JULIET: So you're serious about helping them to set up a centre in England?

DONALD: They asked me to be Patron, my dear. One could hardly refuse.

(A silence falls between the two. DONALD stands patiently awaiting developments, JULIET takes another drink from the bottle)

DONALD: Juliet, please, throw that bottle away and come inside.

JULIET: I'm enjoying it and there's still some left.

DONALD: Juliet, that is cheap plonk I use to marinate the more exotic of dishes and to entertain the less appreciative of visitors. Throw it away and we can open a decent bottle.

JULIET: *(Laughing)* You snob. Okay, let's go in. We can put the award on the mantelpiece between the Oliviers and the –

DONALD: *(Interrupting violently)* We shall do no such thing. It is even more hideous than I thought possible. If you insist on keeping it you may hide it in the cupboard under the stairs with that bloody Oscar thing you refuse to throw away.

JULIET: You are such a snob.

DONALD: Natural refinement and a sense of what is tasteful and what is not, is not snobbishness.

JULIET: *(As they move toward the French windows)* Of course not.

DONALD: You are not irreplaceable you know. I could trade you in for an older, more sophisticated model, who –

JULIET: *(Interrupting as they exit)* Don't push your luck, Donald, I still have a bottle in my hand.

DONALD: *(Off)* Ah, a totally reasonable point from a truly mature and sophisticated – ow!

A week later. The French windows are closed, the kitchen and shed doors open. DONALD *stands beside the table and chairs. He has clearly had another attack and is still in some discomfort though the worst has passed.*

JULIET: *(Entering from the kitchen with a glass of water which she hands to* DONALD*)* Are you going to be all right for this interview?

DONALD: *(After taking several sips from the glass and handing it back)* Of course. The day I fail to dazzle some snot-nosed reporter is the day – sorry.

JULIET: *(Frowning her displeasure but not commenting)* He should be here soon.

DONALD: Good. Looking forward to it actually, it has been a while since I was featured in *The Times*.

JULIET: Try not to let it go to your head too much.

DONALD: My dear girl when a writer of my stature is about to unleash his memoirs on an unworthy public it is only natural that the news hounds should be beating a path to the door.

JULIET: A one man stampede?

DONALD: Don't be impertinent. The rest of the flock will follow.

JULIET: Don't mix your similes, Donald. It's a flock of sheep, hounds gather in packs.

DONALD: News hounds are sheep, and whatever noun they choose as a collective it will soon appear on the doorstep.

JULIET: Naturally. Still, best to start with just the one, eh?

DONALD: The man is from *The Times*, my dear, *The Times*.

JULIET: As in, "that reactionary, right-wing, bottom wiping, lexicon of Murdochese." That *Times*?

DONALD: The same. Not the choice one would have over the tea and toast of a morning, admittedly. But still, *The Times*.

JULIET: And your outburst at their comments on your support for the bypass protesters last year has been forgotten?

DONALD: No, but –

JULIET: *(Interrupting gleefully)* "Authors of a certain age and disposition would be best to continue their hibernation in their own leafy retreats and let progress and development –"

DONALD: *(Interrupting in turn)* Yes, yes, I remember it perfectly.

JULIET: But you're prepared to forgive and forget, so long as they give you some free publicity for your autobiography, hm?

DONALD: Stop it. You know very well that I am a man of the strongest principles. You also know that my support for the campaign to prevent that open wound on the landscape was honest and direct, both verbally and financially. *The Times* was misinformed and the ignoramus who filed the report properly reprimanded. The matter is, therefore, closed and we begin afresh.

JULIET: Just so long as you don't try to use this to have a go at them, you know what'll happen if you do.

DONALD: So long as the issue is not raised, all will be fine.

JULIET: Good. I will be hovering in the background just in case.

DONALD: My dear girl, I do not need a wet-nurse to assist me through a dialogue with some Boy Scout reporter. Senility has not taken a grip yet. I am perfectly capable of performing a simple interview and highlighting several incidents from my distinguished career in anecdotal form for the entertainment of the masses.

JULIET: Of course. Just be gentle with him, that's all.

DONALD: Provided he – *(The sound of the doorbell interrupts him)*

JULIET: That'll be him now. I'll get it. The great one will need time to compose himself.

DONALD: *(As she exits by the kitchen door)* Impudence.

(He positions himself beside the table, one hand resting on a chair back, then shakes his head dissatisfied. He turns his back to the house, standing nonchalantly admiring the view, but again is

dissatisfied. He takes a seat, hands resting on the table, but is still unhappy. He rises and is caught half in, half out of the seat when JULIET *re-enters with the reporter)*

JULIET: Donald, this is Martin Osgood from *The Times*. Martin, Donald Travers.

MARTIN OSGOOD: Mr Travers, a pleasure to meet you.

DONALD: Of course it is, dear boy. I was thinking, perhaps we would be best chatting in my study.

MARTIN OSGOOD: Fine, where ever you're most comfortable.

DONALD: *(Indicating the shed)* Please, after you. Would you care for some refreshment; tea, coffee?

MARTIN OSGOOD: Coffee would be fine, thank you.

DONALD: *(To* JULIET) Would you be so good, my dear?

*(*JULIET *frowns and fixes him with a look before moving off)*

MARTIN OSGOOD: *(From inside the shed)* One of my colleagues was telling me he met you some time ago. Something to do with a proposed by-pass nearby – you may remember the article that appeared? Seems he got an absolute roasting over it.

DONALD: *(Moving toward the shed)* Did he indeed. I am afraid I cannot recall the details, perhaps you could refresh my memory.

(He rubs his hands together and enters the shed)

Mid-afternoon. A few days later. The shed door is closed, the kitchen door and French windows are open. JULIET, *the strap of her bikini top undone, lies face down in the middle of the patio on a large beach towel sunbathing. A tray with a glass and jug of soft drink, and a discarded paperback book, lie next to her.* DONALD *and* SIMON *enter via the French windows.*

DONALD: Tits away, dear, we have company.

JULIET: *(Rising nonchalantly and fastening the strap of her top)* Ever the gentleman, Donald. Simon, good to see you. Drink?

SIMON: *(Recovering from his embarrassment)* No, thank you, I can't stay long. I was just saying to Donald, marvelous piece in *The Times*.

JULIET: Oh, please, don't, I've heard nothing else since it appeared. He even autographed a copy for someone while we were in the newsagent's yesterday.

DONALD: When one is the local celebrity one must expect such things as the norm. We have had *The Observer* and *Guardian* on already and I am expecting several other inquiries. Oh, and the *Daily Mail* telephoned, but I told them to piss off, of course.

SIMON: *(Indulgently)* Of course.

JULIET: Would you like to see his award from the Winsonians, we keep it in a special showroom, subdued lighting, dust covers –

DONALD: *(Interrupting)* Enough! You are supposed to dote on my every word and applaud my every utterance, you objectionable brat. Go and make yourself useful and fetch the papers Simon has come for.

JULIET: *(Dropping a curtsy)* Yes, master. *(She moves toward the French windows and disappears inside)*

SIMON: I don't know how she puts up with you.

DONALD: On the contrary, my dear boy, she is decorative, and occasionally useful, beyond that I often wonder why I put up with – *(Then, as JULIET re-enters, having put on jeans and a T-shirt)* Ah, I was just agreeing with Simon, my dear, I simply could not manage without you.

JULIET: Don't lie, Donald, you were probably saying something nasty about me with which Simon disagreed and are now trying to cover yourself. You're as transparent as that whodunit you keep trying to write. *(Then, as she hands the manuscript to SIMON and before DONALD can respond)* Here we are Simon, the words of the Oracle. I've done my best to ensure you don't get too many actions for libel, but you know how he is.

DONALD: The impertinence of it! I am quite sure
advance orders alone will guarantee it shoots to
the top of the listings.

JULIET: Probably all lawyers in the hope of touting for
business.

DONALD: And my murder mystery will be a shining
example of the genre.

JULIET: Donald, you'd only completed twelve pages
when I told who'd done it. *(Then, to Simon)* He
tried to argue it wasn't who I said it was of
course, but I knew it was, it was *so* obvious. He
hasn't written a word of it since – sheer
petulance.

DONALD: I could always change the victim to his
lordship's young mistress.

JULIET: In that case it would probably have been suicide
brought on by the boredom of waiting for him
to say something original and witty.

SIMON: Game, set, and match, to Juliet, I think, Donald.

JULIET: Thank you, Simon.

DONALD: Pure bias if you ask me. Remember who pays
your ten per cent, my boy.

SIMON: It's twelve-and-a-half per cent, Donald, and I'm
worth every penny. And now, if you'll excuse
me, I must be off. I'll begin this on the train
back and ring you if there's anything of major
concern.

DONALD: Every word is true. Be careful you do not get too engrossed and miss your stop.

JULIET: I'll see you out, Simon. Donald, don't forget you promised we'd call in on Mrs Coogan to discuss opening the Summer Fête again this year. *(She and SIMON move toward the French windows)*

DONALD: Ah, yes, how could I have forgotten. *(Then to Simon)* The burden of being a local celebrity you know.

JULIET: *(As she and SIMON exit)* Of course, he's the *only* local celebrity.

Late afternoon several weeks later. The shed is locked up for the day, the kitchen door and French windows stand open. DONALD, SIMON, DR BRAITHWAITE, and CHRISTOPHER SAYLE sit at the table, a number of papers spread out before them. A tray with discarded cups, bowls, a teapot, and plates of biscuits and sandwiches stands on a serving trolley to one side.

CHRISTOPHER SAYLE: You're quite sure about this, Donald, it really is most unusual?

DONALD: Chris, I have here my solicitor, my agent, and my doctor. Leaving aside the inordinate amounts of my hard earned dosh I pay each of you every year, I consider the three of you to be my closest friends. On that basis, you will agree that I am sound in mind, if not in body.

(The three concur)

Then will you all please sign the damn thing and be done with it.

CHRISTOPHER SAYLE: Very well, Donald, if you're absolutely certain it's what you want. *(He passes a form to* SIMON, *who duly signs and passes it to* DR BRAITHWAITE, *who signs in turn and passes it back to* CHRISTOPHER SAYLE, *who adds his own signature)* There. I'll deposit this back at the office tomorrow. Call me if you need to.

DONALD: You are dashing off then?

CHRISTOPHER SAYLE: *(Gathering the papers together into his briefcase and rising)* Afraid I must. No rest for the wicked.

DONALD: A fair description of your profession. Let me see you out.

CHRISTOPHER SAYLE: No, it's okay. Mind if I use your loo on the way?

DONALD: Of course. You know where it is.

CHRISTOPHER SAYLE: Thank you. Simon, Roger, I'll see you again no doubt. *(They make their farewells as he exits via the kitchen door)*

SIMON: Think I'd best be leaving you to it myself, but tell me, how did you manage to get Juliet out of the way for this? I'm assuming she doesn't know about it yet?

DONALD: No, not yet, the moment has not been quite right.

SIMON: I'm sure.

DONALD: Simon, you talk as if I were not master in my own house.

SIMON: Perish the thought.

DONALD: *(Ignoring the sarcasm)* Juliet has taken herself off to stay overnight with some friends in Eastbourne. I understand they intend to take in a performance of *The Nutcracker*, and then get riotously drunk and disturb the gentlefolk of the neighbourhood.

SIMON: And you don't share her passion for the ballet?

DONALD: I cannot agree with her view of it as a cultural and artistic delight to savour, no.

SIMON: And how do you view it?

DONALD: I find it difficult to see it as anything beyond a bunch of emaciated darlings fannying about in taffeta and tights.

DR BRAITHWAITE: *(Laughing)* The word 'Philistine' comes to mind, Donald.

DONALD: Roger, as you well know, I am a man of the highest cultural and aesthetic tastes; I simply fail to see the appeal, although the scores, of course, may be savored for their own merits.

SIMON: *(Rising)* On that note I think I'll be off. Roger, can I offer you a lift?

DONALD: The good doctor is on night duty, Simon. Having made her arrangements, Juliet, bless her, wanted to have a nurse stay over in case I took a turn. I refused of course, and Roger is the compromise. No offense meant, Roger.

DR BRAITHWAITE: None taken.

SIMON: I see. Well, I'll let myself out. Call you as soon as we have a firm date for publication, Donald, but it'll be in ample time for the Christmas rush.

DONALD: I can already hear the sound of several people choking on their brandy pudding.

SIMON: (Smiling indulgently) Goodbye, Donald. Roger.

DR BRAITHWAITE: Simon.

DONALD: Drive safely, dear boy, and thank you.

(SIMON exits via the kitchen door, closing it behind him)

DR BRAITHWAITE: (After a moment) At the risk of labouring the point, Donald, you're absolutely certain about these changes?

DONALD: Positive. Obviously I do not intend to pop off just yet, but one should always be prepared. It is a matter on which I have thought long and hard. Susan will be well catered for from a number of accounts and investments I have opened in her name over the years, and from the royalties from the continued sale of my various works. Several of the locals also benefit.

DR BRAITHWAITE: Hardly the point I was getting at.

DONALD: You mean Juliet I take it?

DR BRAITHWAITE: Of course.

DONALD: You need not worry yourself; though now removed from my will as recipient of this house and not now otherwise mentioned, Juliet will be catered for in other ways. *(A silence falls between the two for several moments)*

DR BRAITHWAITE: Very well, as you say, it's your will. Before she left Juliet mentioned that you were to be allowed half a bottle of wine this evening. As your physician, I have no problem with relieving you of the other half.

DONALD: Most magnanimous of the pair of you. As a matter of fact, I had a mixed crate of South Africa's finest laid down some time ago. Not had the chance to sample any of them yet. If you would care to deal with that contraption and lead on.

DR BRAITHWAITE: *(As he manoeuvres the trolley toward the French windows)* It must be rather nice to be able indulge yourself like this occasionally.

DONALD: Sometimes, Roger, sometimes.

(He follows after as they exit)

ACT THREE

Late afternoon. Early autumn. The patio is deserted, all doors to the house and shed are closed and locked and no lights are showing. The chairs and table are covered in leaves and the umbrella, which has been removed and furled, stands against the wall. It is clear that the house has been unoccupied for a while. Lights suddenly appear in the kitchen and, after a moment, the kitchen door is opened and JULIET *appears.*

JULIET: *(As she enters)* Sometimes, Donald, you talk through your back trouser pocket.

DONALD: *(Following her out)* Only sometimes?

JULIET: If you're going to throw a tantrum I'll send you straight to bed.

DONALD: If only.

JULIET: Don't be petulant.

DONALD: *(Brushing the leaves from the table and setting a chair upright)* I will not be mollycoddled.

JULIET: Why break the habit of a lifetime?

DONALD: *(Sitting)* Do not be facetious.

JULIET: Why break the habit of a lifetime?

DONALD: *(After several moments and with a heavy sigh)* My love, we have had an absolutely marvellous holiday in one of the few remaining unspoiled cities in Europe, agreed?

JULIET: Agreed.

DONALD: Then please tell me why you felt it necessary to create such a scene at the airport and humiliate me so?

JULIET: Donald, when somebody has a heart attack in the middle –

DONALD: *(Interrupting)* I did *not* have a heart attack. I had a *mild* seizure brought on by arterial inflammation. Roger has explained all this, I have –

JULIET: *(Interrupting in turn)* When somebody has had a heart seizure, whatever the cause, in the middle of the baggage hall at Gatwick airport, it is only natural that it will cause a certain amount of activity. Under the circumstances, it was only natural that first aid be administered on the spot and an ambulance called.

DONALD: I would have thought those people would have been better preoccupied with catching drug smugglers and international terrorists. It was an unnecessary commotion, not to mention humiliating in the extreme.

JULIET: *(Patiently)* Nevertheless, understandable. Taking you to hospital was just a precaution –

DONALD: *(Interrupting again)* Sticking me in a public ward and exposing me to God knows what germs and contagions beggars belief, I would have thought.

JULIET: You'd recovered enough by then to demand a private room, and insist the Consultant contact Dr Braithwaite.

DONALD: Of course I had. If they were adamant on keeping me in overnight for sundry spotty medical students to prod and poke at will, the least they could do was to ensure the dignity and decorum of it taking place in a room of my own, and having all the facts to hand. One hesitates to think what they might have bandaged or amputated otherwise.

JULIET: They are over-worked, over-stressed and, under the circumstances, very tolerant individuals, who are doing their best under difficult conditions.

DONALD: Exactly my point, my dear. And the food. Ye Gods!

JULIET: It was an NHS hospital, Donald, not a five star hotel.

DONALD: That is no excuse for a lack of the basic culinary needs.

JULIET: *(In exasperation)* Oh, you are absolutely intolerable at times. I'm going in to unpack, have a shower, and make something to eat. Do you want anything? Donald?

DONALD: Sorry, my dear, I was just thinking.

JULIET: Yes?

DONALD: If the press happened to get hold of it, could you imagine the headline?

JULIET: *(After a moment)* 'Dicky Ticker Scuppers Scribe'.

DONALD: I was thinking more along the lines of, 'Literary Lion Laid Low', but you get the idea.

JULIET: 'Cranky Creative Codger's Coronary Curse'.

DONALD: Yes, yes, enough. *(Then, as he rises)* You know, that idea of a shower sounds good, leave the cases until later and I will join you.

JULIET: You will do no such thing, you'd be back in hospital in a flash.

DONALD: Are you sure 'flash' is the word you mean to use, in the circumstances?

JULIET: Don't try to be clever, Donald, it won't work. You are not sharing a shower with me and that's that.

DONALD: You can be cruel at times. I am sure one of those nurses would have been far more obliging.

JULIET: *(As they both move toward the kitchen)* Delusions are common at your age, I understand. Mind you, some of the medical students I saw weren't that spotty, quite hunky in fact.

DONALD: You are trying to take advantage of a man while he is at his lowest, stop it.

JULIET: *(As they exit via the kitchen door)* Only a moment

ago you were wishing I *would* take advantage of you, make your mind up.

Mid-afternoon. A few days later. The French windows and kitchen door stand open, the patio has been tidied, and the table and chairs reset for use. The window and skylight of the shed are open, the door closed. The sound of typing can be heard. Enter JULIET *via the French windows carrying the afternoon post.*

JULIET: *(Approaching the shed)* Donald. Donald. *(Then, deliberately) Mail* time.

    (The sound of typing stops abruptly)

DONALD: *(From inside the shed) Post,* child, *post.* How many times must I tell you.

JULIET: Calm down, my love, I was teasing.

DONALD: Hmm. Since you have nothing better to do, make yourself useful and open the *post.* Ignore bills and any other such dross, and concentrate on anything which may be of the remotest interest.

    (JULIET *sorts through the jumble of envelopes)*

    Well?

JULIET: Patience, my love. Ah!

DONALD: Yes?

JULIET: White linen-weave envelope with a window – oh, dear.

DONALD: What?

JULIET: American stamp.

DONALD: I sense a certain amount of piss-taking, my
love.

JULIET: On the basis that I think it's from that tart you
were flirting with, you're probably right.

DONALD: On the basis that you are, once again, talking
through your arse, as delectable as it is, and
that I have not the slightest interest in Ms
Benjamin, you may open the letter and read it
to me.

JULIET: *(In a broad American accent as she opens the
envelope)* My darling snuggle-bunny, how I
have missed you deeply. I cannot wait –

DONALD: *(Interrupting)* Obnoxious brat.

JULIET: *(Reading the letter)* It *is* from the she-devil. She is
flying into London – on her broomstick
presumably – in a week's time and wants to
know if you would like to meet for lunch.
Should I write and let her know that newts'
eyes and vipers' tongues are not to your taste,
and you will, therefore, sadly have to pass on
her offer?

DONALD: *(Entering from the shed)* You can tell me why
she wishes to meet, when, where, and whether
or not there are to be others present. Is the
irritating Mr McPhersonn, with two n's and no

discernible conversational topic of note, turning up? Are you invited?

JULIET: She makes no mention of the old codger, nor of me. Presumably she intends a cozy little tryst for two in some candlelit nook.

DONALD: And for why?

JULIET: Doesn't say, just that she is passing through and fancies a little quality inter-personal fondling time with a seasoned stud.

DONALD: *(Snatching the letter from her)* Your glibness is bordering on the jealous, my love. If you have the slightest problem with the thought of my being alone with the woman you may write and inform her I will, most regrettably, be unavailable on which ever day it is. Or you could join us, that *would* be cozy.

JULIET: Regrettably, I'm unavailable on that day. If you want to go, go.

DONALD: *(Reading the letter)* She is suggesting the Friday afternoon, we could make a weekend of it. You could meet up with some of those horrendous university friends of yours whilst I am entertained and find out what she is after – *(Then, as* JULIET *is about to speak)* do not even think of making a facetious comment – then we could stay over until Sunday, catch a show, visit some of the few remaining sights worthy of note?

JULIET: *(After a few moments)* Okay, you've managed to bribe me into letting you loose with the woman, even if you do seem far too keen.

DONALD: Merely curious as to what she has to say. If we are to eat it will have to be La Maison George. A waste of course; the woman's taste buds have probably been destroyed beyond repair by years of sugary drinks and mustard covered hot dogs, or whatever. Still, it is a while since I dined there, and if someone else is paying, why not?

JULIET: I don't know what she sees in you. *(They are interrupted as the doorbell rings)*

I'll get it. Here, *(as she hands him the remaining post)* see if you have any other admirers on the make. *(She exits via the French windows before he can respond)*

(DONALD crosses to the table and takes a seat, idly flicking through the bundle of envelopes, discarding them in a pile on the table without opening any. He reads the opened letter once more then replaces it in the envelope and adds it to the pile)

JULIET: *(As she re-enters followed by* SIMON*)* Donald, it's Simon. I'll make some tea. Simon, Donald has received a love letter from an admirer, if you ask him nicely he'll tell you all about it. Won't be a minute. *(She exits via the kitchen door)*

SIMON: *(Bemused, as he takes a seat)* What was that all about?

DONALD: Ms Benjamin has been in touch.

SIMON: Ah!

DONALD: She has invited me to lunch.

SIMON: To discuss . . .?

DONALD: No, no, I have not yet approached her on that topic. No, this is merely coincidental, she happens to be coming to London, has no contacts there, as I understand, so naturally she would wish a knowledgeable and entertaining dining companion.

SIMON: And she couldn't find one, and asked you instead?

DONALD: You have been spending too much time here of late, Simon, Juliet's less appealing traits are rubbing off on you.

SIMON: Juliet doesn't have any unappealing traits, Donald. How was the holiday? Thanks for the postcard by the way.

DONALD: Excellent, excellent, we had a marvelous time.

(JULIET *re-enters carrying a tray of cups and other crockery)*

I was just explaining to Simon about your mutual pact of respect and admiration with the delightful Ms Benjamin, my dear.

JULIET: *(As she sets the tray down on the table)* Wash your tongue with soap, you horrible man.

SIMON: Perhaps I'm misreading the situation, but I sense a certain cold response.

JULIET: The woman is a she-devil and is trying to get her talons into Donald. Donald, being totally naive in the ways of she-devils, is in need of my protection and guidance. Excuse me while I bring out the tea and attend to other domestic duties. You carry on with your important men's talk, don't mind me. *(She exits once again before either can respond)*

SIMON: Obviously a delicate subject.

DONALD: Merely a clever ploy. She has already bribed me into taking her up to London for the weekend, doubtless there will be an expensive shopping-spree involved somewhere too.

SIMON: I'm sure she's worth every penny.

DONALD: Of course she is. Just do not tell her I said so, it would only lead to even grander extravagances.

(The sound of the front door bell is heard ringing. A few moments later JULIET re-enters carrying another tray. She is accompanied by DR BRAITHWAITE)

DR BRAITHWAITE: Simon, always good to see you.

Donald, I've brought over the pills I promised, how have you been?

DONALD: (*Taking the bottle of pills as* DR BRAITHWAITE *sits*) Fine, fine, do not start fussing again, it was bad enough in the hospital.

SIMON: Hospital? Have I missed something?

JULIET: (*As she places the tray beside the other and begins to pour the tea*) Donald collapsed at Gatwick Airport –

DONALD: (*Interrupting quickly*) I did no such thing! I merely had a short spasm, was surrounded by a hoard of gawking hoodied Sun-readers, and their snot-nosed brats, on their way home from Ibiza or some such dreadful place, and had to be wheeled away from their clutches by the airport security before I succumbed to the combined odour of stale sweat, cheap beer, and even cheaper perfume. Roger had to rush up to prevent the surgeon from removing a vital organ, otherwise God knows what might have happened.

JULIET: (*Taking a seat herself, having finished pouring the tea*) He collapsed, was unconscious, and woke up in hospital. Donald, you are a total snob and should at least have the decency to be honest with your friends. A 'thank you' to Dr Braithwaite wouldn't go amiss either.

DONALD: Okay, okay. Roger, as you are well aware, you have my unstinting gratitude for your ministering as always. Now, please, it was a great humiliation and an experience I am keen to forget as soon as people stop reminding me of it.

SIMON: But you're okay now?

DONALD: Yes, yes.

SIMON: Juliet, it must have been awful for you.

JULIET: Did put a bit of a damper on things for a while, but he's fine now, that's the important thing.

SIMON: And the good doctor has passed a clean bill of health?

DR BRAITHWAITE: *(With a quick look to* JULIET*)* The tests showed us nothing we didn't already know. The instructions on the bottle are self-explanatory. Juliet, you'll ensure he takes the new tablets?

JULIET: Of course.

DONALD: Will you all please stop talking about me as if I was not even here and drink your damn tea.
(They drink their tea and fall silent for a while)
There, that was not too difficult, was it? I – *(He is interrupted by the sound of the telephone ringing from inside the house)*

JULIET: I'll get it.

DONALD: No, let me answer it, it will give you all the

chance to gossip and get it out of your systems before I return. *(He exits via the French windows)*

SIMON: *(After a moment) Is* he okay?

JULIET: He's fine, just touchy about it happening when it did, it's the first time he's had an attack in public and it upset him, all those people fussing.

DR BRAITHWAITE: Yes, and he didn't take too kindly to being cooped up in a hospital bed for the night. Those tablets I've given him are stronger than the ones he's used to, make sure he follows the dosage correctly.

JULIET: I will. More tea?

DR BRAITHWAITE: No, no, I'm fine. I'll get off once I've finished this.

SIMON: Yes, I'll pop off too. I've brought the first proofs for Donald to go through, unless you'd prefer to have them?

JULIET: Yes, leave them for me to go over and I'll check them through with his lordship later, otherwise it'll take forever.

SIMON: *(Finishing his tea)* Okay, they're on the table in the hall. Let me have any corrections as soon as you can.

JULIET: No problem.

SIMON: *(Rising)* Roger, if you're ready, I could drop you off in the village.

DR BRAITHWAITE: Thank you, yes. *(He finishes his tea and rises)*

(DONALD *re-enters via the French windows*)

DONALD: That was Susan. She and Aslan are on their way, and will be here in about half-an-hour. *(Then, looking at* JULIET*) Someone* has been blabbing.

JULIET: Don't look at me in that tone of voice, Donald, I haven't spoken to Sue for days.

DR BRAITHWAITE: Ah, actually, Donald, I'm afraid I'm the guilty one.

DONALD: You, Roger?

DR BRAITHWAITE: I'm afraid so. Susan rings me every Wednesday and Saturday evening to make sure everything's okay and I –

DONALD: *(Interrupting)* Say no more, it was obviously an unequal battle, I know how intimidating Susan can be. Juliet, my apologies. Please, some tea, this is too much. (JULIET *pours a cup for him*)

SIMON: Roger, I think I should escort you from the premises.

DONALD: Going already?

SIMON: Yes, Juliet's got the proofs to go over, shouldn't be too many problems. Give me a ring when you're ready and I'll pop over for them.

DR BRAITHWAITE: I'll be off too, Donald, give you

some peace and quiet before the others arrive. Looks like you're having a busy day for visitors.

DONALD: Yes, I am thinking of having the drawing room turned into a reception area with a turnstile and so forth. Perhaps you could let me have some twelve month old copies of *Country Life* and *Woman's Weekly* from your waiting room when you have finished with them, Roger?

JULIET: You obviously lost the conversation with Sue, Donald. Don't be bitter. I'll see Simon and Dr Braithwaite out.

SIMON: Goodbye, Donald.

DR BRAITHWAITE: Yes, goodbye. I'll ring in a day or two.

DONALD: Goodbye, goodbye.

> (*The three exit via the French windows.* DONALD *takes a seat at the table and idly fingers the pile of letters*)

> JULIET: (*As she re-enters via the French windows*) *Okay*, go on, get it out of your system.

DONALD: I have no idea what you mean.

JULIET: Bollocks. If you're going to brood all afternoon then I'll leave you to it and you can face Susan alone.

DONALD: Firstly, you would side with her anyway. Secondly, I am fine. I appreciate that you are all concerned for my welfare after such a traumatic and embarrassing event, but I simply wish to forget it and get on with my work. Everyone else, however, seems hell bent on persistently reminding me at every conceivable opportunity.

JULIET: *(Taking a seat beside him)* I'm sorry. I care about you and so does everyone else. It's only natural.

DONALD: *(Heavily)* I know, I know.

JULIET: *(After a moment)* Come on. Help me clear these things away and we'll throw something to eat together for Sue and AsIan.

DONALD: I have never 'thrown' food together in my life, beside which I said we would meet them at the Red Lion for a late lunch.

JULIET: All this hasn't affected your appetite anyway.

DONALD: I just thought Susan might be less vociferous in a crowded room. Although, on second thoughts, as a struggling actress, she might revel in the audience.

JULIET: I promise I won't let her pick on you too much.

DONALD: I am more than capable of fending for myself, thank you.

JULIET: Forgive me, of course I wouldn't dream of speaking for you.

DONALD: You could not possibly speak for me, my dear, you do not know enough words.

JULIET: *(Restraining herself)* I'll let you have that one, Donald, just don't get too carried away. Come on, help me with these.

(The two rise and take up a tray each)

DONALD: Oh, by the way, I think you were wrong about Simon.

JULIET: What?

DONALD: About him being gay.

JULIET: *I* never said he was, it was you!

DONALD: Nonsense, I remember the conversation distinctly. Anyway, he clearly is not. Quite the opposite in fact. Indeed, I think he may be quite sweet on you.

JULIET: Now you really are talking bollocks.

DONALD: I am not.

JULIET: And this sudden revelation is based on?

DONALD: Oh, just some comments he made before.

JULIET: Hmm. You were probably making some facetious remark about me and he, being a gentleman, sprang to my defense.

DONALD: I will say no more on the matter.

JULIET: No, you'll just sit around with that irritatingly smug expression on your face and then slip some stupid remark into the conversation to throw Susan when she's about to put one over on you.

DONALD: Trying to distract me with remarks like that

will not work. I am more than ready for anything my darling daughter chooses to utter, in fact, I am quite cheered by the thought. Lead on, my dear, lead on.

(The two exit via the French windows)

About four hours later. Both the kitchen door and French windows are open and lights are on in both rooms. SUSAN sits at the table reading from some papers. DONALD stands nearby drinking a glass of mineral water without enthusiasm, casting impatient glances at SUSAN as she reads until he can no longer contain himself.

DONALD: Well?

SUSAN: It's brilliant.

DONALD: Of course it is, but do you like it?

SUSAN: Yes, it's wonderful, thank you.

DONALD: Good, then I can send it of to Peter at the BBC with instructions to contact you as soon as he can fit it into the schedules.

SUSAN: You have no problem with accusations of nepotism then?

DONALD: Of course not. Peter has been on at me for a new piece for months and you are the ideal choice for the lead. I said I would write something for you once you had established yourself; had I done so before and pulled strings for you then *that* would have reeked of nepotism. Now you are a young actress with a successful lead in a West End play to your name and the world at your feet.

SUSAN: Hardly.

DONALD: We shall see.

SUSAN: You're up to something. What?

DONALD: I have no idea what you mean. Really, the ingratitude of it all.

(*Enter* JULIET *and* ASLAN *via the kitchen carrying trays of glasses, a bottle of wine, plates of light snacks, and a bottle of mineral water for* DONALD)

SUSAN: Jules, I was just saying how marvelous this is.

JULIET: (*As they set the trays down on the table*) His typing?

DONALD: Impertinence.

SUSAN: Seriously, it's really good.

DONALD: (*Archly*) Good! It is superb.

JULIET: (*Ignoring him*) You'll be marvelous in it.

DONALD: The ideal piece for radio drama.

SUSAN: (*Ignoring him*) Of course, he'll probably tape it and make you sit and listen to it half a dozen times at least.

JULIET: At least. You know, we had to go and see his last play four times in the opening week.

DONALD: There were calls for the author.

SUSAN: (*Ignoring him*) Four! God, Aslan's only been to

see me twice so far. AsIan, you don't love me anymore do you?

ASLAN: *(Laughing)* Ah, discovered.

DONALD: I had to take a bow.

JULIET: *(Ignoring him)* God help us all when this autobiography comes out.

DONALD: Enough! I will not be ignored in my own house. Nor anywhere else, before one of you makes that facetious comment.

ASLAN: *(Making a show of checking his watch)* Thirty-seven seconds, not even close to your record.

DONALD: What are you talking about?

ASLAN: They have a game in which they see how long you can be ignored before you blow your top. The record, and it will take some beating, is two minutes and thirteen seconds.

JULIET: You're becoming far less tolerant in your old age, Donald. Stop it, it spoils our fun.

DONALD: You obnoxious pair of juvenile brats. AsIan, I am surprised at you for encouraging them so, you should be ashamed of yourself.

ASLAN: *(hanging his head in mock shame)* Forgive me, Donald, they made me do it.

DONALD: Stop it now, all of you. You go too far.

JULIET: Stop sulking, Donald. Pour yourself some more mineral water while we see to this bottle of wine. *(Then, as he is about to protest)* Don't even think about it, I told you in the pub that if you drank your quota there you couldn't have any more when we got home.

DONALD: *(As ASLAN and SUSAN sit and JULIET fills three glasses from the bottle)*
But that was cheap pub plonk. The bottle you are dispensing from so freely is older than you are and, given your intolerable attitude at the moment, three times as appealing.

JULIET: *(Sitting)* I know, that's why I chose it. Cheers everyone.

SUSAN: Cheers.

ASLAN: Cheers.

(The three drink and make a show of appreciation)

DONALD: You insufferable bastards.

SUSAN: Language, daddy, there are juvenile brats present.

DONALD: Clearly.

JULIET: Sit down, Donald. Have one of these, Aslan made them. *(She proffers a plate of canapés)*

DONALD: *(Sitting without enthusiasm and taking one of the canapés)* Bas, my boy, while appreciating that you are a vegetarian for admirable reasons and, therefore, refuse to eat anything which has had parents, I do wish you would be a bit more generous with the portions. What is this by the way, I taste garlic and . . .?

ASLAN: Mushroom, parsley, and tarragon.

DONALD: *(Taking another)* Delicious but hardly filling.

JULIET: Don't force yourself, Donald.

DONALD: How is the wine, my dear?

JULIET: Delicious, you should try some sometime.

DONALD: I will bear the option in mind.

SUSAN: He's going to sulk again.

DONALD: Stop it.

SUSAN: Sorry, daddy, dear. Are you going to come and see me again when you come up to London?

DONALD: *(Distracted as he helps himself to another of the snacks)* What?

SUSAN: Jules mentioned that you were coming up to London again shortly; something about getting your hands on an antique American organ-grinder, whatever that is. Anyway, I wondered if you were coming to see the play again?

DONALD: *(Glancing at JULIET and receiving a broad smirk from her)* We may well do so. The meeting I have is of no real importance, a courtesy more than anything, and we will be making a weekend of it. *(Then, as he takes the last of the canapés)* These really are delicious, Bas. Anymore?

ASLAN: Eh, no, they all seem to have gone. I could –

JULIET: *(Interrupting)* You've had enough all ready, Donald. *(Then, before he can respond)* Don't argue.

DONALD: *(Defeated)* Oh, very well. Yes, given that most of the West End seems to be taken up with bloody singing cats on roller-skates, or another revival of a dusty old Broadway musical, it will actually be a pleasure to see some real theatre. Leave some tickets at the box-office for the Friday evening and we can all go for dinner afterwards.

JULIET: Better not indulge too much at lunch that day then.

SUSAN: *(Puzzled)* Am I missing something here?

DONALD: Absolutely not.

JULIET: Whatever do you mean?

SUSAN: Okay – the two of you are obviously having some private joke which is clearly none of our business so we'll say no more. *(Then, with a sudden involuntary shiver)* It's getting chilly, shall we go in?

JULIET: Yes, it is getting a bit cold. Come on, Donald, otherwise we'll have to get out the hot water bottle and wrap you up in a couple of blankets.

DONALD: Do not push your luck, my dear.

JULIET: As if I would.

> *(The four rise, taking up the trays, glasses etc. between them and move toward the house. As they exit via the French windows the sound of a sudden rain shower is heard)*

Mid-morning about ten days or so later. JULIET, *an envelope in one hand, stands at the open French windows waiting for a rain shower to blow itself out. The door and skylight of the shed are closed, the window, through which can be heard the sound of typing, is open. After a few moments the rain stops and* JULIET *moves toward the shed.*

JULIET: Donald, you have a letter from the she-devil. *(Then, as the typing continues and there is no response)* Donald! I know you can hear me.
(The sound of typing stops)

DONALD: What? What is it?

JULIET: You have a letter. It's from the she-devil.

DONALD: *(Entering from the shed)* I do wish you would stop calling her that. The first five or six times were slightly amusing, now it wears thin. *(He takes the letter)*

JULIET: Should I go about my household duties and leave the two of you alone?

DONALD: You really are determined to persist with this. I would have thought, following my lunch appointment with the woman and the grilling you gave me afterwards, that you could not have the slightest remaining doubt about my total disinterest in her.

JULIET: She is, despite her shallow intellect and irritating mannerisms, an attractive woman.

For her age.

DONALD: Agreed, but hardly relevant.

JULIET: So you would not be interested if circumstances were different?

DONALD: Absolutely not.

JULIET: But if she were the last woman on earth?

DONALD: I would demand a recount.

JULIET: Then, unless the letter declares her undying infatuation and her inability to live without you, we will consider the matter closed.

DONALD: Good.

JULIET: *(After a few moments)* Aren't you going to open it then?

DONALD: I thought you had some chores to see to?

JULIET: *(Laughing)* Bastard.

DONALD: *(Opening the letter)* Ms Benjamin writes to thank me for my sparkling, her word, company and hopes I enjoyed the meal. As I chose both it and the restaurant, that goes without saying.

JULIET: Naturally.

DONALD: Please, do not interrupt. Blah, blah, blah, she has returned to Philadelphia, blah, blah, blah, hopes to come to London again before Christmas, and could she possibly impinge on my company again then?

JULIET: How sweet. Where the blah, blah, blahs, merely blah or *blah*?

DONALD: Just blah. One would think the woman was living some sort of double life.

JULIET: That would be two more than I thought she had.

DONALD: Enough. Be gone with you and let me get on with my work so that I can earn enough to keep you in the decadence you demand. What time is Simon due?

JULIET: Any minute.

DONALD: Call me when he has arrived and I will see him in the drawing room. Now shoo. Here, file this as you see fit. (*He hands her the letter and returns to the shed*)

JULIET: (*Opening up the letter as she makes to exit via the French windows*) Blah, blah, blah. Hm.

(*As she enters the house she screws the letter up into a ball and tosses it into an unseen waste bin*)

Late afternoon on a surprisingly mild and sunny day a week or so later. The table and chairs are set as if recently used. The kitchen door and window are closed, the French windows stand ajar. The sound of typing is heard through the open window of the shed, the door and skylight of which are also open. The front door bell is heard to ring several times. After a short while KATHERINE enters from stage left.

KATHERINE: Hello. Donald? Hello?

(*The sound of typing continues without pause and*

KATHERINE *moves toward the shed. As she does so,* JULIET enters *via the French windows)*

JULIET: *(Surprised)* Oh!

KATHERINE: Forgive me, my dear, I didn't mean to alarm you. I did ring the doorbell several times but there was no answer so I came around. I think I hear Donald in his little cubby hole.

JULIET: Eh, yes, I was upstairs. In the bathroom. *(Then, loudly)* Donald, Donald, you have a visitor.
(The sound of typing stops and DONALD *enters from the shed)*

DONALD: What is it, I said I was not to be disturbed – *(Then, seeing* KATHERINE*)* Bloody hell!

KATHERINE: Hello, Donald.

JULIET: Oh. *(Then, after a moment)* Your press photographs don't do you justice, I'm afraid I didn't recognise you.

KATHERINE: That's quite all right, my dear. I –

DONALD: *(Interrupting brusquely)* Juliet is being unnecessarily polite, one of her more endearing traits. There is absolutely no reason why she should recognise you. What the bloody hell are you doing here?

JULIET: Donald!

DONALD: What?

KATHERINE: Please, I didn't mean to create a scene. I was speaking to Susan recently, and she mentioned you had had some sort of attack. I was concerned. I simply wanted to see how you were.

DONALD: Susan is an insufferable gossip, not something she inherited from me. If you were that concerned you could simply have telephoned. Quite frankly, I fail to see why you should be bothered.

KATHERINE: I'm sorry. Perhaps it would have been better if I had 'phoned instead of just turning up like this.

DONALD: Or not bothered at all.

JULIET: Donald!

KATHERINE: Forgive me, *(Then,* to JULIET*)* especially you, my dear, simply walking in on you like this –

DONALD: *(Interrupting again)* You always were one for dramatic entrances. And exits.

JULIET: Donald!

DONALD: Will you stop doing that.

KATHERINE: Please, don't argue, please. This is getting out of hand. I simply wanted to make sure you were all right.

JULIET: *(After a few moments silence)* Donald, the least you can do is to say you're okay.

DONALD: I am okay.

KATHERINE: Good. I am honestly relieved.

DONALD: Of course you are. After all, you would never, ever, want to see me upset now, would you?

JULIET: Donald, stop it!

DONALD: *(Ignoring the rebuke)* I assume you did not fly all this way to simply inquire after my health?

KATHERINE: No, I am In London to discuss a production of *The Glass Menagerie,* and to see Susan of course. She's superb, by the way.

DONALD: Of course she is. I would have thought that went without saying.

KATHERINE: You've been to see her?

DONALD: Twice.

JULIET: Look, perhaps I should leave the two of you alone for a while.

DONALD: Whatever for?

KATHERINE: Because diplomacy is obviously another of her endearing traits, Donald. That won't be necessary, my dear, this has obviously been a mistake on my part. I'd best be going.

JULIET: No, please. Donald, there is absolutely no need for you to be so rude. If you're doing it for my sake it isn't necessary, I really don't have a problem with this, and if you're doing it for your sake, stop it. *(Then after a moment)* Look, you two sit down and try not to bite each other's heads off, and I'll go and make some tea.

Okay?

DONALD: Juliet, you know very well Susan and Aslan are due here any minute.

JULIET: Oh, Christ, yes. I'd forgotten.

DONALD: And, of course, you had no idea they would be here.

KATHERINE: Absolutely not. Susan never mentioned that she would be seeing you again so soon when I saw her the other day.

DONALD: And you never told her you would be descending on me like this either?

KATHERINE: Of course not. I didn't even think about it until I got back to my hotel. Susan said you had had some problems and had been rushed to hospital recently. For God's sake, Donald, I couldn't just ignore the fact, could I?

DONALD: *(Reluctantly)* No, I suppose not. Very well, shall we be briefly civilized over a cup of tea before you leave?

KATHERINE: I think that's the best I'm going to get, my dear.

JULIET: I'm afraid so. Please, take a seat, I won't be long. Donald, you've been warned. (KATHERINE *and* DONALD *move toward the table and chairs as* JULIET *exits via the kitchen door)*

KATHERINE: She's very nice, I like her. Susan has told me all about her, of course, and has nothing but praise for her. She certainly seems to have you under control, anyway.

DONALD: Please stop calling her 'my dear', it is incredibly patronizing. Her name is Juliet, as you well know, and –

KATHERINE: *(Interrupting)* Forgive me, we were not properly introduced.

DONALD: My apologies, the moment was somewhat lost amid the sudden shock. Susan and Juliet have become extremely close, almost sisterly, as clichéd as that may sound, and –

KATHERINE: *(interrupting again)* I'm used to clichés, Donald, I used to proofread all your work, remember?

DONALD: I thought we were going to be civil.

KATHERINE: Sorry, Donald.

DONALD: Thank you, and please stop interrupting, it breaks my concentration. Where was I?

KATHERINE: Juliet?

DONALD: Ah, yes. Susan has certainly given you all the details long before now and some of them might even be close to the truth, it has been no secret anyway. Some of the more scurrilous tabloids tried to pry but were soon seen off, and eventually lost interest. As it is, we are perfectly happy and content, and have been so for several years now. She has her irritating habits like everyone else, but one can overlook those – what did you mean, she seems to have me under control?

KATHERINE: Calm down, Donald. It's none of my business, and Susan has always given her approval and support whenever the subject has come up. As long as you are both happy nothing else matters.

DONALD: You were trying to imply I was not in control in my own house.

KATHERINE: Calm down, Donald.

DONALD: I refuse to play silly little games with you. Juliet is obviously curious and is setting up a little session between the two of you, which might prove amusing, or may not, we shall see. Ah, here she is.

JULIET: (*Entering via the kitchen and carrying a tray of cups, teapot, etc*) Well, I see no blood at least. Have the two of you been playing nicely?

DONALD: (*With a look*) What time did my darling tattletale daughter and her long-suffering partner say they would be here exactly?

JULIET: (*Placing the tray on the table and beginning to pour*) Exactly half-past four. But you know what they're like.

DONALD: (*To KATHERINE as he checks his watch*) That gives you exactly thirty-five minutes to drink up, thank Juliet for her hospitality, and perhaps offer a few meaningless, but pleasant, words to me before you go.

JULIET: Donald!

KATHERINE: It's okay, my – Juliet. Please, let me help you.

DONALD: *(As they settle back with their cups of tea)* Well, this is cosy.

JULIET: Enough, Donald, I won't tell you again.

> KATHERINE *gives a knowing smile, which* DONALD *does his best to ignore. They sit in silence for a while)*

JULIET: Well, if the two of you have run out of things to say, let me. You said you might be appearing in the West End, Katherine?

KATHERINE: Yes, I've not appeared there for, oh, eight, nine, years or so. I've just finished filming in New Zealand and I think now would be a good time to do something here. If it comes off, then by the time rehearsals are done with, the film's advance publicity should ensure a good audience for the play.

JULIET: Perhaps we'll come up and see you.

DONALD: I do not believe I am hearing this.

JULIET: Donald, what's the problem? There is no reason why I should resent your ex-wife being here. I really don't see her as a threat and she obviously knew about me ages ago. If Katherine has made the effort to come here out of genuine concern for you, and is comfortable with me, then why are you so bothered?

DONALD: I would have thought the circumstances were slightly different, but my feelings are obviously of no import.

KATHERINE: *(Heavily)* Donald, I am truly sorry for what happened, the way it happened, and for the hurt it caused you. You know I am, I told you often enough. But that was ten years ago for God's sake. We've all moved on a long way since then. At the very least, I would have thought Juliet's presence would –

DONALD: *(Interrupting)* Keep me under control?

KATHERINE: Oh, for Christ's sake! I give up. Juliet, forgive me, this seemed the right thing to do but I've obviously made a big mistake. *(Then, rising)* Donald, you don't deserve her.

(Any further talk is interrupted by the sound of the doorbell ringing)

DONALD: That, presumably, will be Susan and Aslan. This *is* going to be jolly.

JULIET: *(Rising)* I'll get it. Katherine, please sit down, you can't possibly leave now. Donald, you are in so much doo-doo as it is, at least *try* to behave like a grown-up until I get back.

(DONALD *throws his hands up in exasperation.* JULIET *exits via the French windows before he can speak. He and* KATHERINE *sit in silence. Voices are heard off.* JULIET *re-enters with* SUSAN *and* ASLAN *via the French windows)*

SUSAN: Jules, what are you playing at, what's going on? *(Then, seeing* KATHERINE*)* Oh, my God!

KATHERINE: Hello, dear. Aslan.

SUSAN: Mother!

ASLAN: Katherine! What the hell . . .

DONALD: My words exactly.

JULIET: Donald, shut up. Susan, you told your mother Donald had been unwell, she, being concerned, made the decision to come down to see that he was okay for herself. Under the circumstances, and given Donald's habit for self-indulgent over-reaction, perhaps not the wisest move on her part, but considerate nevertheless. Take a seat, I'll open a bottle of wine, I'm sure we could all do with a drink. Aslan, come and give me a hand, we'll need another chair from the kitchen. Donald, tell your daughter how glad you are to see her. *(She exits via the kitchen door,* ASLAN *trailing behind her)*

DONALD: Your mother and I have already agreed that Juliet, should she choose, would not be lost in the diplomatic service. Leaving the three of us alone briefly being the ideal example. You on the other hand, my dear, should be horsewhipped for high treason. Is there anybody you have not discussed my health with? Perhaps one of the tabloids would be interested in your services, I understand there are always vacancies for gossip columnists.

SUSAN: Is that it, or are you just pausing for breath?

DONALD: No, for the moment I am prepared to listen to whatever feeble utterances you care to make.

SUSAN: Thank you. Mother and I, as you are well aware, e-mail each other regularly and talk on the 'phone less regularly. When she said she would be in London for a while it was only natural that she should come to see me perform, and that we should go for dinner and the odd lunch. I pause here to check that your parental egos are both intact and that I am maintaining the delicate filial balance necessary to keep you both happy.

KATHERINE: Fine by me.

DONALD: I have no problems, so far.

SUSAN: Then I'll continue. When we last met the conversation naturally came round to you . . .
(Offering a knowing pause)

DONALD: Naturally.

SUSAN: Mother asked how you were, I told her. Would

you expect me to lie?

DONALD: No, I would not expect that from you.

SUSAN: Good, I merely stated the facts; that you had been having some problems, had been taken to hospital recently, that Jules was adamant that there were no major concerns to get in a twist about. Okay?

KATHERINE: The decision to drop in on you like this was purely mine, Donald. As I said, I only decided to do so when I got back to my hotel. Susan knew nothing about it, and I had no idea she would be turning up here now. There is no conspiracy theory, no ulterior motive, just a genuine concern that you were okay. I apologize for any upset, for any offence, for any anger it has caused. I apologize for the timing, for not ringing, for continuing to breathe the same air as you.

DONALD: Oh, and that was going so well. *(Then after a moment)* I accept your apologies, I do not think it was a good idea to simply drop in, I think it is incredibly unfair on Juliet, despite anything she may say. However, I concede that you would still be concerned despite the circumstances, and that you, Susan, did not act in anything other than a genuine manner.

SUSAN: Thank God for that.

KATHERINE: Good. If you would like me to leave now, Donald, I could do so while the others are still indoors. It would not be a problem and I'm sure everyone would understand.

DONALD: No. No, I do not think that will be necessary. Juliet is taking it all remarkably well and Susan here would only create a scene if you did so, and then Juliet would feel obliged to side with her. They gang up on me something terrible, you know. There are times I barely hold my own, I have to admit, and Aslan refuses to declare his true colours, although it is obvious he knows I – ah, here they are.

(JULIET *and* ASLAN *re-enter via the kitchen door.* JULIET *carries a tray of glasses and a bottle of wine,* ASLAN *two plates of sandwiches, which he places on the table, and a chair, hooked over one arm, which he sets down by the table and sits on)*

JULIET: *(Placing the tray on the table and taking the remaining seat)* So, has peace been declared, or do we have to send for the men in blue hats?

DONALD: No, everything is fine. Katherine and Susan have admitted their mistakes and duly apologised, and I have graciously accepted.

(KATHERINE and SUSAN exchange looks but remain silent)

I notice you are making free with my rapidly depreciating wine cellar again.

JULIET: (*As she pours*) Only the best.

DONALD: So I see.

JULIET: Well, cheers, everyone.

(*Chorus of* 'cheers' *as they each take a glass and drink*)

SUSAN: Did mother mention she might be doing *Glass Menagerie*?

DONALD: (*Taking one of the sandwiches*) She did. Not his best work of course, but quite a pleasing piece.

KATHERINE: And what are you working on at the moment?

DONALD: (*With a look to* SUSAN) Oh, I have just finished my autobiography.

KATHERINE: (*Managing not to splutter on her drink*) What!

DONALD: (*Innocently*) Did Susan not tell you?

KATHERINE: (*With a look to* SUSAN) No, she did not.

SUSAN: Didn't I? How could I have forgotten that?

KATHERINE: I wonder.

DONALD: (*Gleefully*) It is surprising, especially when you both feature so prominently in it. Given your apparent new role as town crier, Susan, you disappoint me.

SUSAN: Enough. I've already had my say on the matter. He refuses to let me see it, and the damn thing is going to be published whatever we say or do, so let's change the subject before the old fart becomes even more unbearable.

KATHERINE: God, the mind boggles. Okay, you vicious old bastard, what have you said about me?

JULIET: Before this gets out of hand and you all become totally unbearable. Let me reassure you, Katherine, I have taken out the less appealing and more offensive ramblings. and Donald's agent and publisher have had their legal people check it over. There are still some quite colourful episodes related, but the people concerned will just have to put up with it.

KATHERINE: Ye gods! Donald, I warn you now –

DONALD: Please, no threats, there is still time for a couple of quick rewrites should I choose to add anything. As it is, I have merely told the fascinating and event-filled story of my life as one of the leading literary figures of the age – the successes, the adulation, the public and professional recognition, the personalities, the occasional wart and all – how is The Dick, by the way?

KATHERINE: That took you long enough to get around to. *(Then, after some moments)* We separated a few weeks ago.

(There is silence around the table)

DONALD: *(After a while)* If you will believe me, I am truly sorry. Irrespective of the pain you caused me, you were obviously happy with the little shit, and I am sorry for you that it has come to an end.

KATHERINE: Thank you, Donald. Not quite the response I would have expected, I admit. Thank you.

DONALD: There would seem no point in gloating; as you said, it has been ten years or so. You have led your life and I mine. Susan, though immensely obnoxious at times, has managed the balancing act between us admirably, I must admit.

SUSAN: *(Ignoring the insult)* Thank you, father.

DONALD: You are interrupting again, my dear.

SUSAN: Sorry.

DONALD: Thank you.

SUSAN: I won't do it again.

DONALD: You recall my using the word 'obnoxious' a few moments ago?

SUSAN: *(Smirking)* Sorry.

DONALD: Shut up, you little brat. Now I have lost my train of thought. Where was I?

SUSAN: Singing my praises as a role model for daughters everywhere.

DONALD: *(Ignoring the comment)* Ah, I remember. Yes,

you have led your life and I have led mine. I am not one for sour grapes, to agonize over the past is to insult the present. You will have observed that I am perfectly happy and contented.

JULIET: Thank you, Donald, that may be the nicest compliment you've ever paid me. Come to think of it, it may be the only compliment you've ever paid me.

DONALD: Enough. I will not be ganged-up on in my own house like this. Aslan, please, say something, you have been far too quiet.

ASLAN: I didn't like to interrupt. *(A chorus of laughter)* More wine anyone?

DONALD: (As *the glasses are refilled)* You see it has not taken him long to make himself at home.

ASLAN: We starving actors have to make do as best we can.

DONALD: *(As he and* ASLAN *reach for the last of the sandwiches, having already eaten most of them between them)* So I see.

KATHERINE: When I asked if you were working on anything, Donald, I was feeding you a line. Susan tells me you have just written a radio story for her.

DONALD: Yes, I always promised to do so, as she has probably told you. It is a diary piece, Susan being the author / narrator telling the story in reminiscences, as it were. I shall not give the ending away, suffice to say there is a clever little twist in the tail.

KATHERINE: I'll probably miss it. Susan, could you tape it and send me a copy?

SUSAN: Of course.

DONALD: And I will send you a copy of my autobiography as soon as it is available, suitably inscribed of course.

KATHERINE: Thank you, I can't wait.

DONALD: If you care to give me The Dick's address I could send him a copy too. Suitably inscribed of course.

KATHERINE: I don't think that will be necessary, I'm sure Richard will buy a copy for himself as soon as he hears about it. Forgive me, can I use your bathroom?

DONALD: Upstairs, third on the left, but the kitchen is over there if you just want to wash your hands.

KATHERINE: Actually, Donald, I need to pee.

DONALD: Ah, the euphemistic Americanism. You have spent too long mixing with the Hollywood crowd, my dear, say what you mean in the first place, it will save so much time. The loo is the second on the left upstairs.

KATHERINE: Thank you, Donald. *(She rises and exits via*

the French windows)

SUSAN: Don't even think about creating a scene while she's gone.

DONALD: I would not dream of doing so.

SUSAN: Good.

DONALD: She will only be gone for a few moments and the scene I have in mind will take much longer.

JULIET: Donald!

DONALD: Silence, child, this is between a parent and his miscreant offspring. Bas, my apologies in advance, it will not be a pretty sight.

ASLAN: Far be it from me to interfere between father and daughter.

SUSAN: Aslan, you wimp!

DONALD: Leave the boy alone, he suffers enough as it is.

JULIET: Donald, a trade off. Leave Susan alone, don't ever mention this again, and I will not make your life hell for the way you've behaved so far.

DONALD: What outrage! I have behaved with the absolute height of restraint and gentlemanly courteousness.

JULIET: Donald! Agree and I'll even let you have some of the next bottle of wine Aslan is about to go and get.

DONALD: *(After a moment)* Agreed – so long as it is a bottle of the '57.

JULIET: Done.

DONALD: Good. Bas, second rack on the right, third shelf down.

ASLAN: (*As he rises and moves* off) Somebody remind me about Independence and universal suffrage sometime.

SUSAN: (*As he exits via the kitchen door*) Behave like a wimp, be treated like a wimp. (*Then*) God, this is surreal. Jules, I had no idea. This must be really uncomfortable for you.

JULIET: Not at all. On the assumption that there is no sub-plot here and that her calling in, the fact she has split up with her partner, and your visit are all coincidental, then why should I be bothered. In fact, I appear to be the only one who isn't uncomfortable with all this.

SUSAN: I assure you, there is no sub-plot.

JULIET: Then everything is fine. I like her.

DONALD: I do not believe this is happening. I see the opening scene of Macbeth unravelling before me.

(*Then, as* KATHERINE *re-enters via the French windows*) Okay?

KATHERINE: (*As she retakes her* seat) Fine. I see you kept your Oscar after all, despite all of your disparaging comments.

DONALD: What?

KATHERINE: The Academy Award you threatened to shove up Richard's arse. I noticed it on the mantelpiece.

DONALD: *(With a glance to* JULIET, *who smiles knowingly)* Oh, yes, next to the Oliviers. Yes, I decided to be gracious, an award is an award after all, even if one does not give it much credence personally.

JULIET: Did you notice the Winsonian Award next to it?

KATHERINE: The which? Oh, you mean the thing with the two pigeons or whatever? Yes, I read about it in the papers.

JULIET: *(Ignoring a broad laugh from* DONALD) Donald is very proud of all his awards. *(Then, innocently)* You've never won an Oscar have you?

KATHERINE: No. No, I lost out for the film for which Donald won his, and again last time I was nominated a couple of years ago.

(Re-enter ASLAN *via the kitchen carrying a bottle of wine which he has opened)*

ASLAN: *(Placing the bottle on the table and re-taking his seat)* There we are.

KATHERINE: *(After a moment)* Donald, is everything okay, why are you making those faces?

DONALD: I have some blasted vegetation caught between my teeth.

KATHERINE: Oh, is that all. Here, give them to me.

JULIET: *(As the others' laughter subsides)* I must remember that one.

DONALD: *(Refusing to be drawn)* Please remember, you are still a guest here, Katherine.

KATHERINE: Actually, Donald, to be serious for a moment, I've just had an interesting thought –

DONALD: *(Seizing his chance)* Really? Not like you.

SUSAN: Touché, Mother. I've been keeping score here and you're still way behind on points.

KATHERINE: Really? I didn't realise it was a competition. Of course, it would be pointless trying to match your father's devastating wit and enormous intellect anyway.

SUSAN: Point to you.

DONALD: Susan, please be quiet and listen to the obvious sense in your mother's last sentence before you think of interrupting again. *(Then, to KATHERINE)* You were saying?

KATHERINE: I was just wondering, is *Hide and Seek* on anywhere at the moment?

DONALD: I believe it has just finished a run in the Midlands somewhere, Nottingham perhaps? And there are a couple of productions in Canada. Oh, and one in Australia, I think. Why?

KATHERINE: I went to a performance while I was in New Zealand, Auckland, actually, and – forgive me, I was going to say I'd forgotten how good it was, but that wouldn't be possible, of course.

(SUSAN *wets a finger and draws a figure one in the air*)

DONALD: *(Ignoring her and speaking again to KATHERINE)* Presumably this is leading to something?

KATHERINE: I was wondering if you would consider allowing me to produce a version? I'm about right for the lead and Susan would be ideal for the role of Cathy.

SUSAN: Mother, that's brilliant! Father, you have to say yes.

DONALD: *(After a moment's thought)* Given that you are both actresses of considerable skill, am I to believe that this notion is completely spontaneous and not something the two of you have plotted and are now trying to sell me on with a prepared performance?

SUSAN: The idea!

KATHERINE: Donald, totally out of the blue, I swear.

DONALD: *(Again, after a moment's thought)* Hm, it *is* an interesting idea. Juliet, what do you think?

JULIET: Sounds great, why not. When were you thinking of doing this?

KATHERINE: God, I don't know. I've got *The Glass Menagerie*, Susan has a few things going on.

Perhaps we could look to the New Year.

DONALD: Certainly.

JULIET: Perhaps you should sort it now, while you're all here. Donald, we could let Simon know and get him working on the necessary paperwork.

DONALD: Fine, let him earn his corn. Katherine, you are staying at the Savoy presumably?

KATHERINE: Of course.

DONALD: Then I will get him to contact you there.

SUSAN: Brilliant! Appearing with my mother in a play written by my father.

DONALD: Calm down, my dear, these things are not so simple as all that, there is a lot to be done yet. *(Then, to* KATHERINE*)* I could have a word with Derek Whitlock and see if he would be willing to direct, unless you had a director of your own in mind.

KATHERINE: No, Donald, you go ahead.

DONALD: Good. I will have a word then get him to contact you. Bas, my boy, what about you, you have hardly said a word since you got here. What have you been up to?

ASLAN: Not much. I missed out on a film part I was keen on, but I may have landed a role in the pilot for the new BBC series about Mountbatten.

DONALD: Excellent. Perhaps we could fit you in to this

little family project we seem to be developing? If Susan is to play the defendant and Katherine her lawyer, perhaps you could take on one of the supporting legal roles? I have a certain influence and may be able to pull a few strings.

ASLAN: *(Joining in the general laughter)* Thank you, that would be great.

SUSAN: Well, it's certainly been an afternoon for revelations and surprises.

DONALD: Yes, I think I have earned the dinner you are so generously treating us to – on which subject, Katherine, can we avoid a potentially embarrassing moment, or do we have to be polite and ask you to join us?

KATHERINE: No, no, I should be going anyway, it's a nice drive back and I still have a few calls to make. Susan, presumably you and Aslan are staying over?

SUSAN: Yes, it's cheaper than the hotel in the village, although the landlord isn't quite as nice.

DONALD: I shall ignore your impudence and simply add another bottle of wine to our order.

JULIET: You will do no such thing, you've had enough all ready.

KATHERINE: *(Rising)* Ah, I want no part of this. Donald, I'm glad everything is okay. Juliet, you've been the perfect hostess. It's been really nice to meet you, my apologies again for simply dropping in like this.

JULIET: *(As the two shake hands)* Not at all, I enjoyed meeting you.

(Hugs and kisses are exchanged between KATHERINE and SUSAN and ASLAN)

SUSAN: Perhaps I should see you out, mother.

KATHERINE: Fine, I'll call you in a day or two. Donald.

(After a few moments awkward hesitation the two exchange a brief hug and kiss on the cheek. KATHERINE and SUSAN exit via the French windows while the others resume their seats)

JULIET: Anything you'd like to get off your chest before Susan comes back?

DONALD: Other than to say that you have been incredibly understanding and tolerant, no. The touch with the Academy Award was pure genius, by the way.

JULIET: Thank you, Donald.

DONALD: Though you will put it and that other monstrosity back in the cupboard before we go to dinner.

ASLAN: Did I miss something, or should I not ask?

JULIET: Don't ask.

ASLAN: Fine.

DONALD: You are okay about Katherine and I possibly working together?

JULIET: Sure.

DONALD: Very well, it has all the makings of a huge hit, I must admit.

(Susan *re-enters via the French windows*)

SUSAN: Well! Juliet, under the circumstances I think you've earned dinner. *(Then, as she resumes her own seat)* Father, you were intolerable.

DONALD: What! You impertinent –

JULIET: *(Interrupting)* Enough! Let's not start this again. Sue, Donald was just saying how much he's looking forward to working with you all.

SUSAN: Yes, great isn't it.

DONALD: Although it is to be hoped your mother does not bring with her to the stage any of the irritating habits and penchant for excessive demands she has undoubtedly picked up in Hollywood. You know what those people can be like unless they are kept firmly in check.

JULIET: Donald, just once – Look, there is about a glassful of wine left in that bottle. It's yours, and I'll even let you have an extra glass over dinner if, just once, you can say something complementary about my fellow Americans. You have five seconds.

DONALD: *(Weakly after several moments of deep thought)* At least they are not French.

JULIET: Feeble, Donald, feeble, but probably as good as

it'll get.

(DONALD *pours the last of the wine in to his glass and drinks it with relish*)

SUSAN: Well, at the risk of repeating myself, it's been quite an afternoon.

ASLAN: Yes, I don't know about the rest of you but I for one am looking forward to an enjoyable dinner out.

DONALD: Oh, have you not dined out recently. I thought the two of you were avid restaurant goers?

ASLAN: Actually, Katherine treated the two of us the other night. Unfortunately, we couldn't decide between Indian and Greek, so we spent two hours looking for a restaurant called Zorba the Sikh.

DONALD: *(To* JULIET *over the general laughter)* I sincerely hope, under the circumstances, you are not going to be your usual officious self and embarrass me with your 'you cannot eat thoses' and 'do not choose thats'.

SUSAN: Jules only has your best interest at heart, father.

DONALD: Rather a poor choice of words, my dear.

SUSAN: Oh, shut up, you cantankerous old sod.

DONALD: Oh, cutting, cutting. At least your mother instilled a degree of wit in to her banter.

SUSAN: Oh, now she's gone you're going to start on her?

DONALD: Not at all. As I have already said, it was a shock to see her, simply walking in as she did, and I admit it threw me for a while. That said, it has served a useful purpose in that one was able to be civil and courteous to her face-to-face, and she likewise – to the degree that we may now work together again. I would have thought that in itself was worthy of your praise.

SUSAN: Okay, well done. It's a big weight off my shoulders and I'm proud of you both.

DONALD: Thank you. The bitterness and animosity I bore your mother was superseded some time ago by my feelings for Juliet, perhaps it simply needed something like this to clear the air.

JULIET: My God, two compliments in one day.

DONALD: Make the most of them, they may need to last you a while.

SUSAN: *(After a few moments)* She was saying that the press haven't got word of the split yet but they'll probably have a field day when they do.

ASLAN: Inevitable I suppose. Thankfully there was no one else involved, just a mutual decision.

DONALD: Thank you, my boy, I had a certain curiosity, I must admit. Though I am sure she will find a suitable padded shoulder to cry on.

SUSAN: Stop it.

DONALD: And one does have to feel sorry for her;

imagine having to celebrate another fortieth birthday by herself.

SUSAN: Stop it!

JULIET: Donald, enough.

DONALD: Forgive me, I had them on standby, and did not get the chance to use them.

SUSAN: Any more cheap shots, or can we move indoors and discuss something else?

JULIET: It is getting a bit chilly.

DONALD: My God, quick, before she brings out the woolly cardigan and knitted scarf to wrap me up in.

JULIET: *(Laughing)* Stop it. I bought some old clothes from the local charity shop to make up a guy for Bonfire Night and he was convinced I'd got them for him.

DONALD: *(Moving toward the house)* She would have me bedridden and befuddled like something out of Chekhov if I did not assert myself. As my daughter you should keep an eye on her, you know.

SUSAN: *(As she, JULIET and ASLAN gather the plates, bottles, glasses etc. between them)* Stop moaning or we'll dress you up and put you on the bonfire.

ASLAN: In certain parts of India it was not uncommon for the women folk to throw themselves on the funeral pyre of the man of the house.

DONALD: Well said, my boy, there is hope for you yet.
Although I always had rather a fancy for –

JULIET: (Interrupting) Could we change the subject.

SUSAN: Yes, let's talk about something a bit more interesting, like my portrayal of Cathy the supposed mass poisoner in the forthcoming West End smash hit.

ASLAN: Don't they find her guilty and send her away for thirty years?

SUSAN: Shut up, Aslan.

(They all exit via the French windows)

Early evening a week or so later. The shed is locked up and the table and chairs set as if unused for a while. The kitchen door stands open and lights from there, the drawing room and some of the upstairs windows cast long shadows across the patio. SUSAN emerges from the shadows. Without a coat she huddles herself against the cold and looks pale and drawn. Enter JULIET via the kitchen.

JULIET: How're you feeling?

SUSAN: Christ, Jules. I had no idea he was this bad – I mean, this is frightening. How can you manage, day after day, it must be –

JULIET: (Moving closer and putting an arm around her) Stop rambling. Most of the time he's perfectly all right. Occasionally he has some mild problems that feel like no more than a bad bout of indigestion, sometimes, like now, it's more serious. He'll be fine, honestly. Just let him rest. Doctor Braithwaite has given him something to help him sleep, and Aslan's boring the arse of him with a story he's forgotten Donald actually told him.

SUSAN: I've just never seen him like this before. He looks so weak and . . .

JULIET: That's it, isn't it? It's the shock more than anything. The attack he had at the airport was far worse than this, and you saw how he responded then.

SUSAN: I suppose. God, I'm sorry, I haven't even asked how you are, we just jumped in the car and flew down.

JULIET: A flying car, there's a novelty.

SUSAN: Stop it. How are you?

JULIET: I'm fine. I –

DOCTOR BRAITHWAITE: *(Entering via the kitchen)* Ah, there you are.

SUSAN: How is he?

DOCTOR BRAITHWAITE: He's asleep. I don't know which worked quickest, my sedative or Aslan's story. I'm sure Donald has told me that one himself at least three or four times.

SUSAN: Can I go back up, just for a minute?

DOCTOR BRAITHWAITE: Yes, why don't you. AsIan is feeling a bit lost by himself.

(SUSAN *hurries indoors via the kitchen*)

JULIET: *(After watching* SUSAN *exit)* So, now that we are alone, how is he really?

DOCTOR BRAITHWAITE: Lucky, very lucky, this one could have killed him. His heart is very weak. Very weak.

JULIET: So you're saying he doesn't have long left?

DOCTOR BRAITHWAITE: No, not long.

JULIET: How long?

DOCTOR BRAITHWAITE: A month, two, maybe. Impossible to say for sure, but he wouldn't be able to survive another attack like that. *(Then, after a moment)* We really should move him to a hospital –

JULIET: *(Violently)* No! No! You said yourself that there was nothing anyone could do. I won't have him waste away like a rotting vegetable. If it happens – when it happens – so long as it's quick . . . *(She stops, unable to continue)*

DOCTOR BRAITHWAITE: Technically, Susan is the next of kin, you know.

JULIET: Are you threatening to tell her?

DOCTOR BRAITHWAITE: No. But, should she ask, I would be duty bound to tell her straight.

JULIET: Lie.

DOCTOR BRAITHWAITE: You know I can't.

JULIET: *(Heavily)* I'm sorry. God!

DOCTOR BRAITHWAITE: *(Moving closer)* You can't go on like this, Juliet, for your own sake.

JULIET: Oh, I think I can manage another month or two. After that you can lock me away in a rest home for as long as you want.

DOCTOR BRAITHWAITE: Please, don't. You have to remember, Donald is a friend as well as a patient, and I've known him now for a long time.

JULIET: I'm sorry, this can't be easy for you either.

DOCTOR BRAITHWAITE: Watching this happen makes me feel so useless.

JULIET: I really can be a bitch at times. Forgive me?

DOCTOR BRAITHWAITE: Of course.

JULIET: *(Letting out a long sigh and gazing up at the sky)* Does it make any sense? I really don't want Sue, or AsIan, to go through this. I just don't want them to have to cope with the mess of feelings that I am.

DOCTOR BRAITHWAITE: I do understand, really. I might even agree with you as a friend, but from a professional point of view I –

JULIET: *(Interrupting)* I know, I – please, just don't say anything unless you really have to. Please.

DOCTOR BRAITHWAITE: I'll just carry on as I have

been. *(Then)* Should we go in now, before you freeze?

JULIET: You go ahead, I just need a minute to myself.

DOCTOR BRAITHWAITE: Okay. I'll just pop up and make sure everything is all right, and say goodbye to Susan and Aslan. I'll call back in the morning, about nine-thirty?

JULIET: Fine. And thank you.

DOCTOR BRAITHWAITE: You make sure you get some rest. Promise me.

(JULIET *nods her head in agreement*)

Don't be too long.

JULIET: I won't. It's just sometimes . . .

(*After* a *moment* DOCTOR BRAITHWAITE *exits via the kitchen door. As soon as he is gone* JULIET *holds her head in her hands and bursts in to a flood of tears*)

ACT FOUR

Late afternoon. Early winter. The patio is deserted. A light shows from the window and skylight of the shed, which are closed, as is the door, though the sound of raised voices can still be heard from inside. Lights also show from various windows of the house, the French windows stand partially open. The kitchen door is closed. The table, chairs and umbrella have been set away. The shed door bursts open and JULIET appears, obviously in a temper.

DONALD: *(From inside the shed)* Sometimes you go too far. I will not be treated like a bloody three-year-old child.

JULIET: At least a three-year-old child has the excuse of being three years old for its actions.

DONALD: Enough.

JULIET: *(Growing conscious of the cold)* What are you going to do, hold your breath until I give in? Doctor Braithwaite told you clearly –

DONALD: *(Interrupting)* Roger is a fussing old hen –

JULIET: *(Interrupting in turn)* Oh, picking on me isn't enough, now you have to insult your best friend. You're an insufferable old –

DONALD: *(Interrupting again)* Stop it! Please.

(There is the sound of movement from within the shed as if someone is manoeuvrering with difficulty.

After a moment DONALD *appears. He is using a wheelchair and looks pale and haggard)*

All I ask is that you do me the dignity of remembering that, while I may be restricted to this bloody thing for the moment, I still have all my faculties about me. I do not need spoon-feeding, I do not need my arse wiping for me, I do not need to be talked to in words of one syllable v-e-r-y s-l-o-w-l-y and with an imbecilic grin on the speaker's face, I do not –

JULIET: *(Interrupting again herself)* Okay, calm down, I get the picture. All I'm asking is not to be blamed for the ignorance and prejudices of others. I know this is difficult for you, I know, and I'm doing the best I can to help –

DONALD: *(Interrupting yet again)* Oh, stop waffling wench and make yourself useful. The Master is cold. Come on, shut up and take me indoors before we freeze our various extremities off.

(JULIET moves to close the shed door before manoeuvrering the chair toward the French windows. DONALD tucks his hands deep into his pockets. As they near it begins to snow)

JULIET: Any more outbursts like that and I'll let your tyres down, jam your breaks on, and leave you out in the middle of the garden.

DONALD: Callous bitch.

JULIET: Geriatric old fart.

DONALD: Cruel, heartless, harpy.

JULIET: Wizened old –

DONALD: *(Interrupting)* Ah, you used 'old' again, I win.

JULIET: I let you.

DONALD: Liar.

JULIET: Shut up, you *old* codger.

DONALD: *(As they manoeuvre indoors)* Looks like it will snow for a while, leave me by the window and put Bing Crosby on the gramophone, I am feeling decidedly festive again.

JULIET: We have neither a gramophone, whatever that is, nor any Bing Crosby records, as you well know.

DONALD: Pity, pity.

> *(JULIET closes the French windows and DONALD sits watching the snow fall)*

Mid-afternoon, Christmas day, a week or so later. The shed is closed up, lights show from several windows of the house. Both the kitchen door and the French windows are closed. JULIET, well wrapped up, is putting the finishing touches to a snowman. SUSAN opens the French windows. Bing Crosby's White Christmas is heard from inside the house.

SUSAN: *(Leaning half-out)* Jules, we're here.

JULIET: Sue! Merry Christmas. Can you believe he's got

me doing this.

SUSAN: *(In a passable imitation of Donald)* Christmas isn't Christmas without a snowman. *(Then, as the two laugh)* Come in before you freeze, I –

(She is interrupted as DONALD appears behind her, urging her out into the open, followed by ASLAN. SUSAN and ASLAN exchange hugs and kisses and seasonal greetings with JULIET. DONALD leans against the door frame. He is clearly in jovial spirits but still looks somewhat gaunt)

DONALD: *(To JULIET)* I thought you would have finished that by now. Bas, lend a hand there. Susan, there is a cauldron of spiced punch bubbling away in the kitchen, bring a jug full and some glasses. Go, go.

JULIET: *(As SUSAN exits back indoors and ASLAN moves to help JULIET)* If you're going to stand there giving orders, Donald, go and put a coat on. *(Then, as he is about to speak)* And a scarf. *(Then, again before he can say anything)* And a woolly hat and mittens.

DONALD: *(With a smile)* Do not push your luck, my dear, seasonal good will stretches only so far.

(He disappears indoors)

ASLAN: How's he been?

JULIET: *(Reflectively)* Better. Yes, a lot better. That last attack really knocked the stuffing out of him, he's been really subdued – gets frustrated and impatient, more with himself than me – not the Donald of old, no tantrums or blustering, but, well . . . *(Her voice trails off. Then)* This has bucked him up though, he's always like a big kid at Christmas.

ASLAN: Yes, I see he's got all the presents under the tree as usual.

JULIET: Oh, yes. I have to buy him a special present to open just after midnight otherwise I'm awake all night making sure he doesn't sneak down and unwrap everything.

ASLAN: What did you get him?

JULIET: I toyed with the idea of a zimmer frame, but he wouldn't have thought it funny.

ASLAN: *(Laughing)* No.

JULIET: Half-a-dozen things came to mind but in the end I decided to be boring and predictable and got him an expensive, a very expensive, bottle of brandy. Worked out quite well, he had two glasses, fell straight asleep as soon as he got into bed, and slept for ten hours solid.

(SUSAN enters via the kitchen carrying a tray on which is a steaming jug of the punch and four glasses, already filled)

SUSAN: Where is the old sod?

ASLAN: Jules sent him to his room to put his winter woollies on.

SUSAN: Good. How's he been?

JULIET: Fine. I was just saying to Aslan, all this's got him behaving like a five year old.

SUSAN: No change there then.

DONALD: *(Reappearing at the French windows in overcoat, scarf, heavy gloves and something resembling a deerstalker hat)* What are you all twittering about?

JULIET: Nothing. What *do* you look like?

DONALD: Silence you impertinent brat. Susan, why are you just standing there, give me one of those.

SUSAN: *(Distributing the glasses of punch and setting the tray down)* Certainly, father dear. What *do* you look like?

DONALD: Enough. Aslan, my boy, the ground looks treacherously slippery, lend me an arm.

ASLAN: *(Knowingly)* Of course. By the way, what *do* you look like?

DONALD: *(Raising his eyes to the heavens)* I despair at times.

SUSAN: *(As they all sip their punch)* Oh, before I forget and if it's of any interest, mother sends her best wishes to you both.

JULIET: That's nice of her. We went to see her by the way. I really enjoyed it, and I thought she was excellent.

SUSAN: I'll pass that on. Father?

DONALD: Yes, yes, yes.

SUSAN: What does that mean?

DONALD: Yes, I enjoyed the production, yes, I thought your mother was excellent in the role, and yes, you may pass on my regards. Okay?

SUSAN: Thank you, I'll let her know.

DONALD: *(Removing his hat and tossing it to* JULIET*)* Good. If you have finished there you can add that, I found it at the back of the wardrobe, and then we can all go inside so I can finally open my presents.

JULIET: *(Catching the hat and placing on top* of *the snowman)* There, now he looks just like you.

DONALD: Impudence. Come on, Roger will be here soon, and Mrs Williams at the *post* office informs me he received a not inconsiderable parcel the other day. One assumes it can only be a case of wine to help replenish my diminished reserves.

JULIET: Poor Doctor Braithwaite. You don't deserve his friendship the way you treat him.

(SUSAN takes up the tray and they all move indoors via the French windows)

Early morning. A few days later. The kitchen door stands open. JULIET *is shoveling snow from the patio. The shed door, window and skylight are closed but the sound of typing can be heard from within. Enter* SIMON *via the kitchen.*

JULIET: Simon! Merry Christmas.

SIMON: You too.

JULIET: This is a surprise, we weren't expecting you. You should have said.

SIMON: All a bit of a last-minute rush I'm afraid. Got caught up at JFK Airport in a twenty-four hour strike – threw everything out. *(Then)* Even forgot to bring the mistletoe.

JULIET: Oh, you don't need that. *(She moves forward to give him a hug and a long kiss on the cheek)*

SIMON: *(Recovering)* Eh, Susan let me in, said Donald was out here?

JULIET: Yes, he's sorting out his Christmas mail; thank-you letters to the adoring masses, as he puts it. There aren't that many so he shouldn't be long.

SIMON: I won't interrupt him yet then. *(Then, after a moment)* Is it my imagination or does that snowman resemble Donald?

JULIET: *(Feigning surprise)* You know, it hadn't struck me before, but now you mention it. I must tell him.

SIMON: *(Alarmed)* Oh, no, please. You know –

JULIET: *(Interrupting)* Simon, relax, I was only teasing.

SIMON: *(Relieved)* Oh.

JULIET: You really shouldn't let him intimidate you so.

SIMON: I –

> *(They are interrupted as the shed door opens and DONALD appears)*

DONALD: Juliet, I need you to – Simon, good to see you! I thought you were slumming it in New York for the holidays? A belated Merry Christmas, and a Happy New Year in advance.

SIMON: Thank you, you too. Problems with flights and so on, flying out again on the third so I thought I'd pop down and visit. Nice to see Susan and Aslan.

DONALD: One has to be kind to one's less fortunate relatives at this time of year.

JULIET: *(Leaning on her shovel)* I'll tell her you said that.

DONALD: Be quiet. *(Then to SIMON once more)* Come in and see the pile of letters I have received from people whose festivities have been enhanced by reading my life's story. Any news by the way?

SIMON: Still number one on the non-fiction list and a runaway success in the States too.

JULIET: How you dare to call it non-fiction is beyond me.

DONALD: Be quiet.

SIMON: I've brought a whole stack of letters with me which the publishers received, and those that came to my office as well.

DONALD: Juliet, we shall need more stamps.

JULIET: You made me buy five hundred, that's more than enough.

DONALD: Be quiet. Simon, come in out of the cold before I catch pneumonia. Juliet, idle hands, idle hands.

(As DONALD and SIMON disappear into the shed JULIET hoists the shovel as if a spear and makes to throw it at DONALD. Shaking her head and smiling she returns to clearing the snow. After a few moments she examines the immediate area and, satisfied, lays the shovel aside. As she does so SIMON and DONALD reappear)

JULIET: *(To SIMON)* See, I told you it wouldn't take long.

DONALD: Be quiet. Simon neglected to say that he has brought presents for us both. Under the circumstances letter writing can wait. Simon, even though Juliet has done her best, this still looks decidedly slippery. Lend me an arm, dear boy. We can open the new presents and I can read the fan-letters you have brought while the women-folk and Aslan prepare something to eat.

JULIET: We will do no such thing, you've only just had breakfast; you can wait until lunch time. *(Then, as* DONALD *is about to speak)* And if you dare to tell me to be quiet once more today I'll take that shovel and . . . *(there is no need to finish the sentence)*

DONALD: Juliet, Simon has travelled all this way, the least we can do is feed him.

SIMON: It's okay, I had a bite on the way down.

DONALD: Be quiet. It would be remiss of me as a host, particularly at such a festive time to –

JULIET: *(Interrupting)* Donald, be quiet. Simon, you are more than welcome to join us for lunch, which will be in exactly – *(she makes an elaborate show of checking her watch)* three hours.

SIMON: I'd be delighted, if it's not too much trouble.

DONALD: My god, we will starve.

JULIET: *(Ignoring him)* Not at all. Let's go in and swap presents. I chose yours so you'll really like it. Coming, Donald? *(She leads the way toward the French windows. SIMON hesitates until DONALD, defeated, places a hand on his shoulder and the two follow)*

DONALD: *(To SIMON as JULIET opens the French windows)* To quote William Morris, one should not have anything about the house which is not useful or decorative. Luckily for Juliet, she is both.

JULIET: *(Exiting)* I heard that.

Mid-afternoon. A week or so later; a few days into the New Year. The shed door, window, and skylight are closed, as are the kitchen door and French windows. Enter JULIET *via the French windows. She hurries to the shed.*

JULIET: Donald, I can't find them anywhere. Donald.

DONALD: *(From within the shed)* Well they are definitely not here. Could you try again, maybe in the bureau on the landing? They must be somewhere.

JULIET: You are a senile old fart.

DONALD: But you love me nevertheless.

JULIET: Of course.

DONALD: Then run along before I forget the fact.

JULIET: *(With a smile and a shake of the head)* Check under that pile of magazines in the corner. *(She crosses to the French windows and exits. There is the sound of movement from inside the shed)*

DONALD: Juliet, it is okay, I have found the damn things. Juliet? Juliet? *(After a moment, there is the sound of more movement then the sound of typing. A few moments later the typing stops, then starts and stops again several times)* Shit! Juliet!
(The sound of movement follows after a brief silence)
(Desperately) Juliet! – Oh, Christ! – Juliet! – Jul –!
(Then a loud crash. After a while JULIET *reappears.*

She is carrying a number of envelopes)

JULIET: *(Approaching the shed once more)* Donald, I've checked the bureau and there's still no sign of them and Sue has rechecked the bookcase in the hall. *(She pauses to pick out one of the letters)* The *mail's* arrived. Looks like you have another love letter from the she-devil. Donald. Donald? *(Then, with sudden alarm)* Donald? *(She moves toward the shed door)* Donald! *(Then, in a scream of horror as she opens the door)* Donald!

As at ACT ONE, *first scene.* JULIET *enter from the shed and closes the door behind her on a Yale or similar lock. She is wearing an overcoat, scarf, and cloche hat and is carrying a large cardboard box filled with various unidentifiable items.*

JULIET: Sometimes, people ask me how I ever got myself into such a situation – as if I had no say in the matter, as if it were something I had no control over. *(She pauses, setting the box down)* God! If I'd known it would end like this . . . *(She glances around her briefly, shaking her head, then picks the box up again and exits via the kitchen door closing it behind her. After a few moments the door reopens and* JULIET *reappears. She notices that the shed window and skylight are still open)*
Shit!

(She crosses to the shed, opens the door and disappears inside. After a moment the skylight is closed, then the window. As she reappears and is locking the shed door again SIMON *enters stage left)*

SIMON: Juliet?

JULIET: *(Turning in sudden alarm)* Jesus! Simon, you scared the crap out of me!

SIMON: Sorry, sorry. I couldn't see any lights on so I came round the side. I'm sorry, I didn't mean to frighten you – stupid of me – sorry . . .

JULIET: *(Recovering her composure)* It's okay, just a bit of a shock. Everything's been switched off for weeks, I couldn't be bothered turning it back on. I'm only here for a few minutes, collecting some bits and pieces. *(Then)* What are you doing here anyway?

SIMON: I came to find you.

JULIET: What? Why?

SIMON: Been trying to catch up with you for weeks, but no one knew where you were. Thought you'd come back here at some point, so I've been coming down as often as I could and staying over in the village. Someone saw you drive past by chance and told me.

JULIET: I don't understand, there was really no need for you to worry.

SIMON: Of course there is, but that's not the main reason.

JULIET: I don't understand.

SIMON: It's to do with Donald's will.

JULIET: Simon, really, Donald made it perfectly clear who got what and why. I don't have a problem with it, honestly.

SIMON: No, sorry, I'm not explaining myself very well. *(He rummages in an inside pocket, finally pulling out a large envelope and offering it to* JULIET*)* Here.

JULIET: What is it?

SIMON: It's from Donald –

JULIET: *(Interrupting)* From Donald? *(She takes the envelope)* I . . .

SIMON: He gave it to me ages ago, when he altered his will and cut you out of it. I didn't understand at the time, but he was adamant I should give it to you as soon as – when – if anything happened. That's why I've been trying to catch up with you, it's obviously important and . . . *(He falls silent as* JULIET *takes a letter from the envelope and reads it to herself)*

JULIET: *(After several moments)* The bastard! He knew!

SIMON: What?

JULIET: He knew. He knew he was dying. I thought I'd

managed to keep it from him and all the time he knew.

SIMON: *(Confused)* I had no idea.

JULIET: Doctor Braithwaite and the specialists told me last year and I didn't want him, or anyone else, to know. He says nobody told him, that I shouldn't go looking for anybody to blame, and that I really shouldn't have tried to insult his intelligence by playing games with him, but he understands why I kept everything to myself, and thanks me for not burdening Susan, or anybody else. *(Then, reflectively)* The bastard.

SIMON: *(Again)* I had no idea. God, what you must have gone through.

JULIET: *(Taking something from the envelope)* Like he said, there was no reason for everybody to go through it. What's this? *(She examines the object she has removed from the envelope)* Jesus! Oh, God!

SIMON: What is it, what's wrong?

JULIET: This; it's an account book for a building society, in my name – with – with two hundred and thirty-two thousand pound in it.

SIMON: Good God. I –

JULIET: *(Interrupting)* Wait, there's another note. *(Then, as she reads)* He repeats what he said in the will – that he didn't think it would be fair to expect me to take on the house and grounds by myself

– *(Then, with a brief laugh)* and that he could not bear the thought of it being bought up by some intellectually deficient snot-nosed juvenile from the City – he wasn't allowed to state that in the will – so giving it to the Winsonian Society seemed the obvious solution. He apologizes again for any upset this has caused, and . . .

SIMON: And*?*

JULIET: And hopes that Simon has not been too lackadaisical in getting this to me. Only Donald would use a word like lackadaisical, and spell it correctly.

SIMON: Juliet, I'm really sorry, I –

JULIET: Simon, shut up. There's really no need. God, I don't believe this. At least everything makes sense now. Sort off.

SIMON: Juliet, I'm really sorry, but after the funeral you just disappeared, I had no idea where you'd gone or –

JULIET: *(Interrupting absently as she returns the notes and account book to the envelope)* I flew to the States – my mother's.

SIMON: Of course, I should have thought.

(They fall silent for a while)

I'm glad things have sorted themselves out for you. I knew Donald must have been up to something when he made the alterations to his will. *(Then after several moments)* What are you going to do now? Go back to the States?

JULIET: Possibly. I had intended to – this changes things a bit. Perhaps I'll finish my Masters. I could do a paper on the life, works, and legacy of Donald James Travers, author, poet, playwright, intellectual giant, and wit . . . *(Her voice trails off as she struggles to compose herself)*

SIMON: *(Moving forward instinctively then hesitating before placing a hand on her shoulder)* Juliet . . .

JULIET: *(Recovering)* It's okay. Sorry.

SIMON: No, take it easy. *(Then)* Christ, what you must have gone through.

JULIET: *(Reflectively)* It's strange, but once it happened everything seemed to go on automatic pilot; the undertaker, the paperwork, the funeral. It's a process that just runs its course and you have no control, you just get pulled along with it. *(Then, after a moment)* I managed to have a quick word with Susan at the funeral before I dashed off, I'm afraid I just needed to get away from it all.

SIMON: That's okay, it *was* a bit of a circus.

JULIET: Wasn't it. Donald would have loved it, the crowds, the press, all those literary and acting celebs, even some minor royalty. I thought your eulogy was wonderful.

SIMON: Really?

JULIET: Yes, Donald couldn't have written it better himself.

SIMON: (As *the two give a brief laugh*) Praise indeed.

JULIET: *(After a moment)* God, that's the first time I've laughed in weeks.

SIMON: You sound relieved.

JULIET: it is a relief, I mean, the time's just flown over and I can't even say I've been doing anything. My mother's been great, just let me be there, no interference, no smothering, just there when I needed a shoulder.

SIMON: That's what mothers are for. Did she ever meet Donald?

JULIET: Yes, a couple of times, once over in the States and then we invited her over here for a couple of weeks. Once she got over the fact that he was older than she was everything was fine. You know what an absolute charmer Donald is – was. Shit.

(The tears come despite herself)

SIMON: *(Moving closer to place an arm round her shoulder)* Hey, come on.

JULIET: *(Wiping her eyes but staying within his hold)* I'm fine, just give me a minute.

SIMON: *(Drawing her nearer)* Take all the time you need.

JULIET: *(After a while)* There, fine now, just needed to get it out of my system.

SIMON: Can't be easy for you, coming back here like this.

JULIET: No, no, actually it's okay. I – I suppose I had been putting it off – but once I got here it was fine. This house has always been so cosy and – it – it was no problem.

SIMON: You said you were picking up a few bits and pieces?

JULIET: Yes. I 'phoned the Winsonians a few days ago to find out what was happening – the plans sound really good. They're turning the house into accommodation for the staff and visiting lecturers with study rooms and a library, and a new block in the paddock is going to be dormitory accommodation for students, and workshop, seminar, and lecture areas.

SIMON: Yes, I've been liaising with them quite closely.

JULIET: Of course. Anyway, I asked if I could come and collect a few things I'd left and pick up some personal items of Donald's. They've been really good about it. When do they move in?

SIMON: Next week. They're keeping Donald's study as it is and turning the garage block into a sort of memorial museum with his papers, note books, photographs, and awards and so on.

JULIET: Sounds good, Donald would love the idea of

that, I know.

SIMON: I'm sure he would.

> *(They fall silent each lost in some personal thoughts. After a few moments it begins to snow)*

We'd best be moving.

JULIET: Yes, I've stacked a few boxes and bags in the hall.

SIMON: *(As she moves toward the kitchen and he begins to follow)* I'll give you a hand.

JULIET: Thanks.

SIMON: *(Hesitantly)* Look, if you don't have to dash straight off, perhaps we could call into the pub for a drink. Have you eaten?

JULIET: *(Pausing)* No, no I haven't. Yes, that would be nice. Thank you.

> *(The two exit via the kitchen door, SIMON closing it behind him. After a moment it opens again and JULIET reappears. She stands for a while and there is, perhaps, the faintest echo of a practiced and steady typing as she gazes out at the patio and grounds beyond as the snow continues to fall)*

> JULIET: *(After a moment)* Sometimes, Donald. Sometimes . . .

> *(With a final look about her she closes the door)*

CURTAIN

Kevin Cowdall's writing is hypnotizing

About The Author

Kevin Cowdall was born in Liverpool, England, where he still lives and works. In all, over 200 poems have been published in journals, magazines, and anthologies, and on web sites, in the UK and Ireland, across Europe, Australia, Hong Kong, India, Canada, and the USA, and broadcast on BBC Radio and RTÉ Radio, Ireland.

His 2016 retrospective collection, *Assorted Bric-à-brac* brought together the best from three previous collections (*The Reflective Image*, *Monochrome Leaves*, and *A Walk in the Park*) with a selection of newer poems). His most recent collection, *Natural Inclinations*, features fifty poems with a common theme of the natural world.

His poem for children, *The Land of Dreams*, was published on the Letterpress Project website, wonderfully illustrated by Chris Riddell.

Kevin's novella, *Paper Gods and Iron Men*, and his novels *The Ghost in the Room*, and *Cosgrove's Sketches*, have received excellent reviews.

**All of Kevin's books are available on Amazon
in hardback, paperback, and e-book
(Except *Cosgrove's Sketches* – e-book and paperback only)**

By The Same Author
Cosgrove's Sketches

Novelist Michael Powell is approached by the eighty-one year old Catherine Coburn to write a novel based on the short but eventful life of her father, the Edwardian artist, Meredith Arthur Cosgrove.

Between 1923 and '24 Cosgrove produces *The Three Graces* paintings: studies of a young woman bathing, for which he becomes both famous, for their composition, and infamous, for the story behind them. The model for all three – the seventeen year old Emily Coburn. By the time the first painting was begun the two were already lovers, by the time the third was finished, Emily was pregnant by the thirty-nine year old artist. Disowned by their families, the scandal which ensues forces the two to move to Paris, where their daughter is born. They are immediately adopted by the city's Bohemian community, meeting the likes of Ernest Hemingway, James Joyce, Pablo Picasso, Ford Madox Ford, Man Ray, and Gertrude Stein.

Using her father's 'visual diaries' – annotated sketchbooks of people he met, places he visited, little scenes that took his fancy, and also her mother's, Emily Coburn's, journals. Michael Powell writes the story, as factually-based as possible, with key historic events and principle characters instantly recognisable, but with an elaborate fiction woven around them – narrative 'moments' which develop the relationship between Cosgrove and Emily until the key moment: *'when they looked in to each other's eyes and knew that their lives were about to change irrevocably.'*

Cosgrove's Sketches is a family saga, a historical evocation, a contemporary literary narrative, a comparative social commentary, a Bohemian idyll. Above all, it is a love story.

The Ghost in the Room

In a London hotel room, Ian Kincaid, The Ghost, ex-SAS- / MI6-trained renegade, relates a series of 'case files' to journalist, Patrick Walker, detailing various assignments he has undertaken for clients, targeting international terrorists, human-traffickers, neo-Nazis, arms-dealers, drug-smugglers, paedophiles . . .

'You want a personal mission statement? Okay . . . I do bad things to bad people who do bad things to good people.'

★★★★★ A great read that will keep you guessing 'til the end. If you love action stories, you'll love this. Kevin Cowdall has created a fascinating character with some incredible tales to tell. A thoroughly enjoyable read.

★★★★★ Brilliant thriller! Really enjoyable novel. Given how each chapter relates a different 'case file', this would make a great TV series on Netflix or Sky. In the meantime, a highly recommended read.

★★★★★ Brilliant read. Absolutely loved this book. It's a cracking read. Kevin keeps you guessing right to the twist in the end.

Paper Gods and Iron Men
(with *Flanagan's Mule*)

A single three-bladed fan turned slowly in the centre of the ceiling, barely disturbing the scorching air which filled the small prefabricated hut like an oven ...

Set in the North Africa Campaign of World War II, the novella, **Paper Gods and Iron Men**, is a story of endurance and survival, of ordinary people in extraordinary situations.

Two British Army officers have come together at a temporary aerodrome to be flown out. When their plane is shot down the two are the only survivors and begin the long trek north across the desert ...

Published with the short story, **Flanagan's Mule**, which shares the theme of personal determination and resolve, and which is set in a South-American mining community in the 1950s.

★★★★★ Tremendous new voice.
These are two wonderful stories of survival. Cowdall has an expertly controlled style and is a tremendous new voice. At times I was reminded of the early, and best, Norman Mailer.

★★★★★ An epic journey of survival.
Intensely-felt and beautifully-written story of determination and grit. The author plunges his readers into a world which he imagines and describes with great vividness. At one level, this is a classic war story, but it is Kevin Cowdall's prose which makes it something special. The writing varies from terse and gruffly masculine to poetic. Recommended to all who have ever imagined themselves on an epic journey of survival.

The Ophelia Garden

A Collection of Ten (and a bit) Short Stories

This collection brings together ten (and a bit) of my earlier stories, several set in a time before the Internet, mobile-phones, and, dare I say, e-books.

These are tales of prophetic newspapers and predictive magpies, late-night hitchhikers and telephone stalkers, childhood sweet-hearts and lost loves, curiosity, resentment and fixation, affairs, passion, lust, and red lace panties.

Most are works of pure fiction. A couple are, to a degree, semi-autobiographical. All are intended as mere self-contained narrative whimsies, written with no other purpose than to entertain.

★★★★★ Unexpected Tales!
I was most reminded of Roald Dahl's *Tales of the Unexpected*, with perhaps a dash of Martin Amis.

★★★★★ A different offering from Kevin.
Sometimes it's nice to read a complete story before bed. This collection fits the bill. I particularly liked *Not Drowning, But Waving*.

★★★★★ A great set of short stories.
This collection by Kevin Cowdall really fits the bill of what you want from a short story: a quick, but not always light, read that often leaves you wondering, and delivers a few surprises.

Assorted Bric-à-brac

A retrospective anthology of 50 poems

★★★★★ A lovely collection of poems, like finding a perfect shell on the beach – unexpected and beautiful.

★★★★★ Wonderfully reflective poems, full of vivid images and descriptions.

★★★★★ Like music for the soul.

★★★★★ A collection to dip in to again and again.

Natural Inclinations

50 poems with a common theme of the natural world

★★★★★ Brings poetry and the world of nature together in perfect harmony.

★★★★★ A wonderful collection. Full of vivid and evocative images.

★★★★★ Fabulous collection of poems about wildlife.

★★★★★ A delightful collection. Thoroughly enjoyable and highly recommended.

Printed in Great Britain
by Amazon